Mystery
of the
Vamours

NEW BEGINNINGS

MERCEDES HUBERT

Published by Richter Publishing LLC www.richterpublishing.com

Book Cover Design: Jessie Alarcon

Editors: Sarah Harder, Skylar Rainey & April Avis

Book Formatting: Monica San Nicolas

ISBN: 978-1-954094-21-5

DISCLAIMER

CONTENTS

ACKNOWLEDGMENTS

I would like to express my gratitude towards all those who have given their time and efforts to help/support me as I brought this long overdue tale to a reality. First and foremost, I would like to thank Courtney D. Armstrong for the countless hours she put into reading and rereading my work. You inspired me along this journey in a way that forced my own creativity to shine through. Another huge thanks to Tonya Arcangeli, who pointed out my story flaws and helped me develop my monsters throughout the book. I would like to also thank my amazing husband Aaron Hubert, whose patience with me during this process is immeasurable. Final thanks to my incredible publisher Tara Richter at Richter Publishing, who pushed my story to entirely new lengths.

INTRODUCTION

Life was supposed to be simple. I had it all planned out. All I had to do was study, work hard, and act normal and I could be successful in life. Doesn't sound too terribly difficult. That is, unless you're me. Which is why I shouldn't have been surprised when I found myself one night shortly after my sixteenth birthday hiding in a panel in our wall with my mom and my uncle, a man I had only met days before. Just outside the door, heavy footsteps stomped around my home, tossing our belongings like they meant nothing. Between the crack of the panel and the frame of the wall, I finally caught a glimpse of the thing that had hunted me my whole life. It was shaped like a man but was at least three times as large. It had no neck and a small head when compared to its body. Its heavy breathing was all I could hear. I gasped, and it swiveled towards the closet.

My uncle threw the door open, pinned the monster down on the ground.

"Run to the barn!" he yelled as the monster shrieked.

My mom and I fled the house, sprinting across the yard to the barn. We just made it, pulled the doors shut, and locked them. We turned, looking for something to barricade it when a man came up from behind. We shrieked and shrank back against the door as he approached.

"It's ok! I'm a friend of your uncle," he said. "I'm here to help, but we need to go now."

"What about him?" I cried. "We can't leave him!"

"He'll be fine, he can handle himself," the man said.

"Anya, we've got to go, we've got to go now," Mom said. We fled the barn, piling into the man's black Suburban. We drove through town, past its outskirts, and kept going.

"Where are we going?" Mom asked.

"I'm taking Anya to a safe house," he said.

"I'm going with her!" Mom cried. He didn't respond.

"Mom is coming with me!" I said. He just nodded.

We pulled up to a private runway, hidden between hayfields in the middle of nowhere. He drove through the field and stopped next to a small jet waiting on the track before getting out. It was dark outside, and the moonlight was all we had to see with. There were some lights on inside the small plane, and when the door was opened, lights lit up the stairs. As we were getting ready to board, my uncle drove up in a small car. He was covered in dirt and wet from something. I got in the plane while Mom was talking with him. I waited a few minutes, but Mom never got on. I got up to see what was taking so long and made it to the door when I saw my uncle holding my mom back. He had his arms around her waist, holding her from behind as she kicked and screamed for me. He was dragging her back to the dark Suburban.

"What the hell are you doing?" I yelled, panicking. The man who drove us started walking towards me up the steps into the plane.

"She can't go with us. Those are the orders," he said, blocking my path off the plane. I went to push him out of the way, but someone from behind grabbed me. I was dragged to my seat and held like a prisoner. A man explained that only I could go and my uncle would take care of my mom until I could see her again. I began to panic and hyperventilate. I could see the lights turn on along the runway as the plane turned on its loud engine. I saw my uncle outside the window pushing my mom into the vehicle. I tried kicking the man holding me back as I continued to scream until the plane left the ground.

1

BACK TO THE BEGINNING

There are two things you need to know about me. The first is that I was adopted at a very young age. I don't remember my biological parents. My new mom, Grace Lee Harris, adopted me when I was two. She's an incredible mom—tall with long, brown wavy hair, soft spoken and kind-hearted. She is always willing to help anyone in need, even if she doesn't have it herself to give. One time when I was little, Mom took me to her work, and on our way, we came across a homeless family. We didn't have much money back then, but she still stopped at the store and bought blankets, water, and snacks for them. I remember how full my arms were carrying the blankets.

We lived in Bellthorpe, Queensland, Australia on a small hobby farm with a cute two-story house that my grandparents built in the early 1940's. It had worn, grey wood planks on the outside and an old, creaky wrap-around porch. The windows were so old that most didn't even open. It could have used some repairs, but it was perfect for just the two of us. Our neighbors had cows that we shared our land with, and we had some chickens that roamed the yard. Our property was fenced, with a large, red wooden barn out back. It was an old hay barn with some horse stalls on the main level. The chicken coop was in the barn, in an old stall from when we once had horses.

My mom was a zoo guide at the local zoo about forty-five minutes away in Landsborough. I loved listening to her talk about all sorts of animals at the zoo. That's what got me so interested in animals. She also was my homeschool teacher, as if that doesn't say enough about my social life. I used to go to public school when I was younger, but I never got along with the other students. I seemed to be an angry kid and remember throwing a lot of tantrums at school. I hated sharing and had a hard time playing with others. The other kids always thought I was odd or strange, so they would pick on me. The teachers usually blamed me because the other kids would have bad things happen to them when they teased me, and they would say I did it. Mom felt I was being bullied too much. The teachers felt I was the bully, so Mom decided she would just homeschool me instead of arguing with them all the time.

The second thing you need to know about me is that mysterious things happen around me. One time on the bus when I was seven, two girls took my backpack and were taking my homework out and ripping up my papers. I got so angry I started to scream. That's when a big gust of wind blew through the bus, stirring the papers all around. The bus driver yelled at me to close my window, but I never opened it. It did scare the two girls enough to leave my stuff alone.

Another time I was being bullied on the playground by a classmate named Justin, who was hitting me with soccer balls. I got down into the fetal position because he hit me in the face, and I began to cry. Suddenly the ground vibrated, and Justin was pelted with a bunch of small rocks. I was the one who got into trouble for throwing rocks at him, even though I hadn't touched anything. I would argue with the teachers for things I didn't do and would get into more trouble for lying. I was becoming angrier as I grew up because I resented everyone. Once I got into middle school, Mom had enough and pulled me out to be homeschooled.

Every day began the same. Usually, Mom woke me up for breakfast or I would smell it from bed and come running. I would wait around the house to say goodbye to her before she left for work. Then I would go out exploring. Our home was next to Bellthorpe National Park where I loved to explore. It felt like I was on a new adventure every day. Sometimes I would check out the crocodiles. Other days I would check on the kangaroos. I loved taking my camera with me and shooting my own documentaries on all the different animals I came across. I did schoolwork in the afternoons when Mom got back from work.

Our lives were not perfect, but I was happy. Mom would constantly nag me to try to meet some of the local kids at the park in town. She would always say I needed more friends, but I was happy with how things were. The strange things that couldn't be explained still happened to me often, but I wouldn't tell anyone. I found comfort in believing I had a fairy godmother following me. But sometimes it felt like I was cursed and I had a ghost making my life miserable. Mom never saw these things happen, so she never understood what I was talking about when I mentioned it. She always had an answer that explained why things happened.

When I was out filming animals, no one saw the odd things happening around me. During one of my filming adventures, a dingo came out from a wooded area. Once he saw me and I saw him, we both froze in what felt like a trance. I felt paralyzed, and my breathing felt forced. That's when I realized I could hear and see everything as if I had switched bodies with the dingo. I never told anyone about what happened to me that day. They would think I was crazy. If this had happened around other kids, they would have made fun of me and called me more names. I told Mom I would try to make friends again though. She always told me that I was older now and had grown a lot since being homeschooled, but I was accustomed to being alone. It still bothered me though, not knowing who I really was. I never truly felt ordinary, even when I tried. Unable to fit in or belong to any social group. I wanted to know where I came from and why these mysterious things happened.

After years of complaining and not knowing my roots, Mom finally had enough. She knew how much it meant to me and finally got on board to look for my biological parents. I'll never forget the day I asked if we could find them. It was before my sixteenth birthday. I was so afraid to ask her—I didn't want her to be mad at me for wanting to know them. But when Mom asked me what I wanted for my birthday that year, I couldn't help myself. I knew it would hurt her, but I went ahead and asked hesitantly. Every year on my birthday, before I blew out the candles, I would secretly wish to one day find out who my biological parents were. After blowing them out, I would wait a few extra seconds before opening my eyes only to be disappointed. Usually after a couple weeks I would give up hope and move on to something else.

But not this year. I had to tell Mom so she could help me this time. She always acted as if she feared that one day, I would leave her behind. As if I would reconnect with my biological parents leaving her behind. I could never leave her though. She was my mom, no matter what the DNA said!

"Can we find my biological parents?" I asked. "I want to finally know where I come from." She put down her newspaper to look at me. I braced myself for the inevitable no.

"Ok," she said.

2

SEARCHING

There I was the next day, not exploring, but gathering chicken eggs out back in the barn. I was lost in my thoughts as I searched for the eggs. It was a windy day, which wasn't good for filming. Sand was blowing all around, and even though it was sunny, visibility was limited when a gust blew through. As I finished collecting the eggs, I thought about going to the library. I could focus in there and get ahead on some of my studies. I kept thinking about the things Mom said to me the night before.

She mentioned that during my adoption many things were left unanswered for her. My biological parents picked my mom out of all the other couples. This was odd to her because she had tried to adopt for years but because she was a single woman she was often overlooked. She also said that my biological parents didn't want to meet her even though she would have thought they would want to meet the person they were giving their child to. She wanted me to be prepared in case we weren't able to find out anything more. I was still excited though, and Mom said she would take the next day off so that we could go to the adoption agency to find some answers.

After gathering all the eggs and getting ready, I walked down the driveway on my way to the library. It was cold, and the sand was pelting me with every gust. The wind was blowing so hard that I kept having to turn away from it because it kept getting in my eyes, but all I could think about while walking to town was how excited I was for tomorrow.

The walk took about fifteen minutes. It was a straight walk to get there and was practically the first building when I reached town, an old red brick building that was a bit run down now. It was always dimly lit inside and smelled like old books. While I was walking up the steps to the front door, it suddenly opened, and the librarian stepped out. Ms. Maggie was happy to see me and rushed me in quickly so she could finish sweeping out the sand. She was a sweet old lady who had run the library since before I started to come about five years ago. I would always go to the same place in the library—the far back corner where there was a desk to work from and a computer to use. It always seemed a bit spooky because of the lighting.

After hours of combing through schoolwork, I felt tired but accomplished. I had finished all of my math work for the rest of the week, most of history and science, and a good chunk of literature. I decided I deserved a break and wanted to go to the park. It was about noon, and I gathered up my belongings and told Ms. Maggie goodbye. The park wasn't far—maybe a five-minute walk. The wind seemed to have calmed down and the smell of food was in the air. Pizza, barbeque and fried fish engulfed my senses and made me hungrier than ever. I had lunch packed, so I couldn't wait to get to the park to eat it. The park was in the center of town and not much larger than a football field. It was more of an oval shape with a walkway through the middle. Sports were played on one side, and the other side was a dog park and a kid's play area. I enjoyed sitting and watching the dogs when I came.

I entered the park and walked a ways down the path. No one else was there. I sat at a bench in the middle and pulled out my sandwich—

peanut butter and jam with the crust cut off. While I sat there, I thought about life and how every kid dreams about being a doctor, fireman, astronaut, or even a pop star when they grow up. I never had that dream. I had always felt like there was something more out there for me, but I wasn't sure what that was. It felt like I had a higher purpose, to do more in this world than I could ever imagine. I felt like I was constantly searching for what I was missing in my life. This is why I needed to find my biological parents and put the missing pieces together.

I looked at the large clock near the entrance of the park and noticed it was almost three. I must have been lost in my thoughts longer than I thought. I needed to start heading home before Mom worried. The walk back was much nicer than this morning. I could hear the birds chirping while I walked without sand blowing in my eyes. The wind had calmed down, and I saw our driveway up ahead. Mom's car was in the driveway, so I knew she was home already. I ran to the house to tell her about all the work I did today. When I got inside, she was acting strange, almost like she was nervous about something. She seemed happy that I got ahead on my work so we could just relax tonight. She wouldn't say what was troubling her, but I could tell something was wrong. Finally, she caved.

"I got tomorrow off work," Mom said. "We can try to find information on your birth parents." I was so excited I hugged her tightly, but she still had a sad look on her face.

"Even if we find my biological parents, you would still be my mom," I said. "You raised me since I was a toddler and you're the only mom I've ever known." I could see a tear creeping down the corner of her eye as she wore a crooked smile on her face.

That night, I barely slept, tossing and turning and checking the time. I just couldn't shut my mind off. I must have dozed off as the sun was rising because that was the last thing I remembered before the sun beamed through my window. Realizing today had finally come, I staggered down the hall and into Mom's room to wake her. I opened her door, but she wasn't there. I rushed downstairs and surprisingly found her sitting and waiting at the kitchen table

"About time you got up," she said, with a smile on her face. It was nearly ten o'clock and I had overslept a tad.

"Well, you seem to be in a good mood this morning" I said, puzzled by her excitement since last night she seemed less eager for this day to get here.

"I know this means a lot to you, filling that void you feel inside. I will do my best to help you. But I want to remind you that there wasn't much information given during your adoption, so I don't want you to get your hopes up either," she said calmly.

"I know, Mom. This means so much to me. I'm so glad you're doing this with me," I said, still excited.

All my life I heard people say where you come from tells you who you will become. Everyone has their own destiny to follow. Knowing where you come from is a large part of what shapes you in the future. I thought knowing who my parents were and maybe meeting them would help fill the void I felt inside. That lost but not found feeling that drove me to keep searching. I loved my mom, but something deep inside me kept telling me I had to find out who my biological parents were so I could understand who I really was.

After we ate a breakfast of eggs and sausages, I got up to go get dressed. Walking away, Mom yelled for me to rinse my plate. I was so excited to get going I had forgotten. We were running behind schedule and should've left already. I ran to get dressed and tripped going up the stairs, stubbing my toe on the last step. Even though my toe hurt, nothing was going to ruin the excitement I had—not even this bruised toe! After getting dressed I brushed my teeth and combed my hair. Mom was already waiting in the car when I went back downstairs. I slipped on my shoes and got in the car. I could feel a knot forming in the pit of my stomach. I had waited for this moment for so long. We pulled out of the driveway and drove down the road towards the big city,

Caloundra. It was over an hour's drive from where we lived. Mom said she had called in advance to make sure we didn't need an appointment.

"Sheila, the woman that answered, said we could just show up," she said. I kept asking Mom if she was sure about that. I didn't want anything to stop us today.

The first half of our trip was mostly farms and trees as we took the scenic route to Caloundra. We weaved through valleys and forests that were thick with trees. To pass the time, we played one of our favorite car games, I-spy. Once we got closer to Landsborough it became more exciting to play in the bigger city area. The drive still felt like it took forever. After about an hour, Mom said we were getting close. The knots were back in my stomach, and I suddenly became nauseous. We were in Caloundra, and every time she turned down a street, I thought we were there.

Finally, we pulled into the parking lot of a government facility building.

"We're here!" Mom said, turning to look at me. Sweating and palms clammy, I had never felt so nervous before.

"Are you ok?" Mom asked. "You look a bit pale."

"Y—ye—yes," I stuttered, unable to say anything else.

We got out of the car and headed inside. The waiting room was empty, and we could hear the receptionists behind the check-in counter gossiping. We signed in and waited to speak to a counselor. One of the women came out to tell us the counselors had gone to lunch and should be back in the next hour. Mom said we could wait. If it took too long, we would go get lunch.

It was nearly one o'clock before we were called back. We followed the counselor down a hall and to her cubical. She began by asking what she could do for us. Mom explained everything to her. I was so nervous I couldn't speak, I just sat there anxiously. She said that she would check the files in the back, but most cases were sealed, and she probably wouldn't be able to tell us much more than that.

Well, great, another dead end, I thought to myself. After what felt like an eternity, but was maybe only ten or fifteen minutes, she returned.

"I was able to find some information after all, Anya," she said. "It turns out your records weren't sealed. However, they are missing. I looked around, but it seems like your file has been misplaced."

"Missing? How is an adoption file missing?" my mom exclaimed. I had never seen her so annoyed before, but she knew how excited I had been. "I called in advance and everything, and we drove over an hour to get here!"

"I really am very sorry, Ms. Harris. We had a break-in a couple weeks ago, and the vandals made a mess of all the files. I'd be happy to make you copies of everything I do have if that would be helpful. And if more pages turn up, I can mail you copies as well."

She handed me the envelope, and Mom said to wait until we got home to see what was inside. I was anxious to know what was in the envelope but confused about how the rest of my records had been misplaced. They didn't just get up and run away. I wondered if my files had gotten mixed in with someone else's when the staff cleaned up.

We thanked the lady and left to go home. Getting into the car, I gripped the envelope, excited to open it. I thought the ride there took forever but I was wrong. Having the information I had waited for so long in my hands and not being able to look at it till we got home was killing me. My sweaty palms left marks on the envelope, but I couldn't put it down. I kept asking if I could just look inside, but Mom wouldn't let me. I just wanted a little something, anything to hold me over till we got home.

"I don't understand why we have to wait until we get home to look," I said.

"Some information in there might need my full attention, and I can't focus on the papers and drive at the same time."

I understood, but I wasn't the one driving, and I sure could read.

"We need to get lunch," Mom added.

I knew she was hungry since she was getting testy about everything. On our way out of the city she stopped for some food. We pulled into a drive thru since it was getting late and Mom wanted to get home. She asked what I wanted, but I really didn't want anything. She ordered first and looked at me, but I still wasn't sure. She ordered me a burger and fries, but I was so excited to get home that I barely ate any of the food. I took a bite of my burger and picked some of my fries. The ride home wasn't any shorter, and it was now three in the afternoon. It felt like we spent most of the day driving. I finally saw our driveway and I realized I had forgotten to turn off the front porch light.

I began to unbuckle as Mom yelled at me to wait till we stopped. I opened the door and jumped out running to get inside. I heard Mom yelling to wait for her as I kicked off my shoes on the porch. I rushed to the table and started to open the mustard yellow envelope. It was sealed with a piece of string around a button. I just couldn't unwind it fast enough. There were about five or six pages inside that I pulled out, and as I did a picture of me as a baby fell out.

"My last name!" I shouted. I finally knew my real name: Vamour. I knew already that Anya was my birth name because Mom had told me she liked it and kept it, but now, I knew I was born Anya Emalia Vamour. The rest of the papers were just about the handling of my adoption and legal stuff I already knew from Mom.

"What about your last name?" Mom asked when she finally came in from the car. "I heard you screaming from outside."

"Vamour, my last name is Vamour!" I kept shouting, excitedly. "I couldn't find anything else but my real last name."

Mom looked through the pages more carefully and found that both Mr. and Mrs. Vamour agreed to the adoption by my mom. The papers only referred to them as Mr. and Mrs. Vamour though, so I still didn't know their first names. The picture that fell out was of me as a baby. The top of the picture was torn off, and it was in black and white. It looked like there were two others in the picture, a man and woman standing behind me, but I couldn't see their faces since the picture was ripped. It made me wonder why they would give me up for adoption if they loved me enough to take a family portrait.

"The pages are numbered," Mom said. "Page one and five through eight are here, but two, three, and four are missing." The lady at the agency was right. I was missing pages from my paperwork.

"The agency will call if they find any more pages," Mom said. "But I'll give them a call in the morning just in case." We went through everything, reading every line to find anything we could. Before we knew it, the sun was going down, and Mom suggested we unwind and watch some television to relax.

I didn't know if I was excited or disappointed after today. I had gone through so many emotions I wasn't sure how I really felt. I was happy to find out my last name but disappointed most of the information was missing.

I had spent so much time searching for answers to who my real parents were, where they came from, and why they left me that I never thought about not being able to find them. I was going to be sixteen tomorrow, practically an adult. Or at least I felt like one. I didn't really want a party or anything but a nice relaxing day. As I was brushing my teeth all I could think about was that my wishes were finally coming true, after years of wanting to find my biological parents. I would finally find out what happened to them. Mom came up to my room to say good night.

"It's going to be challenging," she said. "But we can't give up searching. I won't give up if you don't," she promised.

"All I ever wanted was to just know what happened," I said. "I don't need to meet them or stay with them. I just need to know what happened."

"We'll keep trying," she said. "Goodnight."

I woke up the next day feeling a little bummed out still, but at least I was finally sixteen. I began to smell food, drawing me downstairs. As I went to crawl out of bed, I got tangled up in the sheets and fell on the floor. Instantly, I was stricken with a sharp burning sensation coming from my leg. As I stood up, I realized I had a scrape on my knee. I held my knee up as I made hissing sounds from the pain. I hopped a few steps before realizing it had begun to bleed. I was annoyed, and my knee hurt, but it was still going to be a good day. It was my birthday, and I hadn't even made it out of my room before getting hurt. I headed downstairs where Mom had breakfast ready for me. My favorite—eggs and toast cut up with ketchup.

"Are you alright?" she asked, a grin on her face.

"What are you up to?" I asked mysteriously instead of answering her question.

"I stayed up late last night, posting all of your information on a national database," she said, a large smile now spreading across her face. "Hopefully by spreading the word, people online can try and find Mr. and Mrs. Vamour."

"You're the best!" I said.

"Happy Birthday, Anya. We'll have to plan something, maybe on the weekend."

"That sounds fun," I responded. "Do we have any Band-Aids? My knee is bleeding."

"You klutz," she laughed, leaving to get me some.

For the next few weeks, we got nothing but junk mail and people claiming they knew the Vamours years ago but nothing else.

I started thinking maybe I needed to expand my search for my parents and try to find information myself. If I waited for them to come to us, I might never find the truth. The library would be the best place to start—there were plenty of sites that people posted their family trees on, and I was sure Ms. Maggie would know some of them.

3

SOMEONE'S WATCHING

Despite the excitement about the search for my parents, I continued making trips to the library weekly, at least four or five days a week to do my work. I always sat in the same spot in the back of the library with the computer. It had now been two months since my birthday, and I had begun to lose hope. However, one sunny Tuesday morning, something felt different, and I wasn't sure why. I woke up and did my normal routine, gathered all my things, and left the house. It was an ordinary, clear day as I walked into town. When I got to the library, I went inside and looked around, but no one was there. Even Ms. Maggie, the librarian, was not there to greet me like usual. I walked around and checked through the aisles of books but couldn't find her anywhere. I thought maybe she was in the back where visitors weren't allowed.

I ventured through the library looking at books before going to my usual spot in the corner. There was a crinkled letter taped to the computer monitor where I normally sat. I didn't notice it at first, but after pulling some papers out of my bag, I went to turn the computer on, and there it was. I quickly looked around the room, but no one was there.

The letter was addressed to *Miss Vamour* in messy cursive. My heart was racing. Could this be from my parents? I slowly unfolded the torn piece of paper that was inside. It read:

Dear Ms. Vamour,

It has been years since we last saw one another. You were a toddler and won't remember me, but I remember you. I'm writing this to warn you. You have been putting yourself in grave danger. Be careful, for what you are searching for—it brings great risks. You are drawing unwanted attention to yourself and need to stop searching for your parents. If you still want to know the truth, despite the danger, go to the park. Tell no one.

I paused. Great risks? What an odd thing to write. I wondered what risks there could be in looking for my parents. The writer mentioned knowing me when I was a toddler, which meant they must have known my parents. Who would write this? Was it a joke? *Such a strange letter to find left for me in a public library,* I thought. What if someone else came and sat in my spot before I did? How did this person know I would sit here and not on the other side of the room? I had to know who wrote the letter, so I gathered up my stuff to head to the park.

As I walked through the library to leave, Ms. Maggie came out from the back.

"Ms. Maggie!" I called. "Have you seen anyone else here this morning?"

"No, Anya, I haven't," she said. "How did you sneak in without my knowing?"

"I tried to find you, but couldn't," I said. Ms. Maggie looked at her watch.

"Are you leaving already?" She looked thoughtful.

"I just forgot something at home," I said. I couldn't tell her where I was really going. She walked me to the door as we said our goodbyes.

Walking to the park, I thought about the excitement of knowing something more about my parents or where I was from. The farther I went, the more nervous I felt. I started to get an uneasy feeling in the pit of my stomach. What if this was a prank? Or maybe a trick to get some sort of reward money. Why couldn't I tell anyone where I was going? I could see the park coming up, and no one was around. I hoped there would be others there, but it was Tuesday. Everyone was usually at work or in school at this time.

I started to walk through the park looking around for anyone. It was late in the morning, and the sun was beaming down on me. I got to the bench in the center of the park where I liked to sit near a tree with some shade as I waited. After a while I walked around a few times to escape the heat. I rested and ate my lunch under a tree and watched the birds and squirrels as I fed them my crust. After waiting for several more hours, the sun was beginning to go down. I kept wondering if the letter was just a joke. I knew it—it was just a trick, and I wasted the day sitting in the park. I had seen kids come and go, joggers running through, and people walking their dogs. With each person that passed I got excited and then disappointed. I decided it was time to call it a day and head back home.

As a cool breeze blew through my hair, I got up from the bench and stretched out my arms and legs before leaving. Nearing the entrance, I saw a tall man walking into the park. He looked like he was in his forties, dark hair, and a goatee that was greying. I was passing him when he reached out and touched my arm.

"Anya?" he asked. I looked at him and nodded yes with a questioning look on my face.

"Wow, you've grown up," he said. I was puzzled by his response.

"You know me?" I asked. "How do you know me?"

"I am Aku," he said. "Come, sit, and I will tell you everything." This strange man I just met was acting like he was family. His behavior was very odd to me, yet it left me with a sense of comfort and trust. We headed over and sat on the benches near the entrance.

"I wasn't supposed to look for you," he said. "But I received information on your whereabouts, and heard some demons talking about you. I knew I had to come immediately."

"Demons talking about me?" I asked confused.

"Your parents would have wanted me to keep you safe. I've always protected the family and needed to make sure you were ok. I know you're searching for them, but they need you to be safe." He spoke as if they were close relatives.

"How do you know them?" I asked.

"Anya, I am your uncle," he responded quickly. "Something happened to your parents, and I'm hoping you can help me find them. A few weeks ago, your parents discovered you were looking for them, and they wanted to come find you. But some bad people found them as they were on their way to find you."

"What are their names?" I had so many questions to ask, but I needed to know this first.

"Asa and Amoura Vamour," he said. "How come you don't know that?"

"My mom and I tried looking into them at the adoption agency, but my papers were missing," I said. Aku looked confused but didn't question it.

"Your parents are kind, caring, and giving people, Anya," he said. "They're gifted, and that's what makes you so special."

"I'm special? How?" I asked.

"You're a sorcerer of sorts, what we call a mage," he said. "Some people call our kind witches or magical beings, but we're just like everyone else. Except we possess a power inside us that allows us to do unbelievable things. You were born with magical powers, a gift that gives you the ability to change the world."

The story seemed off the wall, but I listened intently.

"I don't have any special powers," I said finally. "I don't even believe in magic."

"We can test that," he said, looking at me. "See if you have the same gifts as your parents.

Why not? I thought. I had already wasted the day in the park. What would be the harm in a few more minutes?

"Stare at that plastic cup over there on the bench across from us," he said.

It seemed odd, but I did as he asked.

"What's supposed to happen?" I asked as I stared.

"Whatever you want to happen."

I thought about it for a second, before focusing on throwing the cup. *It's all a joke anyways,* I thought. There was no way it would ever work. The man was clearly crazy, and I felt ridiculous. I decided I would stare at the cup just a bit longer and then make an excuse to leave. I thought about the cup and focused on flipping it over. Then, to my surprise, the cup began to vibrate and shake so hard it fell from the bench onto the ground.

"No! No," I yelled, jumping back. "I didn't just do that."

"I know it's hard to believe," Aku said. "Sit, sit. You have your father's gift but favor your mother so much."

I was so confused. I hadn't touched the cup, the wind wasn't blowing, and no one passed by, yet it had still fallen over.

"With training, you could be a grand mage one day, or an archmage like your mother," he said. "There are special kinds of people out in the world that can do all sorts of amazing things. These people are not talked about, and no one knows who they really are. They're a society within a society."

I started to understand what he was saying, but I still found all of this hard to believe.

"Why are you telling me this now, and how do my parents fit into everything?" I asked.

"Amoura and Asa are the only family I have," he said. "Since they went missing, I thought it was best to find you before something else did."

"What do you mean, something else?"

"There are things you won't understand quite yet, but I will explain one day," he said. "Until then, I'll make sure you and your mom are safe."

"Will I see you again?" I asked.

"You might," he said. "I'll be around for a while since you've drawn too much attention."

"Attention from what? What aren't you telling me? Aku, tell me, damn it." Shouting in frustration, I balled my hands into fists.

"Your parents were hunted for trying to share their gift with the world," he explained. "By a demon of sorts who hunts all those with powers like a dog sniffing out rabbits."

"Why can't these dogs be stopped?" I asked.

"Your parents aren't just average powerful people," he replied. "Your dad was the leader of a group of mages that believed their gifts should be shared with the world. Before you were born, your dad killed some powerful demons that stood in his way and that sought to kill him to stop him. Your parents did what they had to do to protect you. They made the hard decision and gave you up for adoption. A few months ago, your parents' guards were taken one by one, and their bodies were found in unusual places. Messages were carved into their flesh, telling us to turn over Amoura and Asa. The guards appeared to have been tortured, and some had limbs torn off. They suffered greatly just to protect your parents."

An overwhelming fear began to overtake me, and I grew chilled listening to Aku.

"It's getting too dark," he said. "You need to go home, quickly. Don't tell your mom about this."

Walking home, all I could think about was sorcery. Did this mean I was a witch, that I was evil? How did I get the cup to fall over? I assured myself that maybe it was a breeze that I didn't feel. Then it dawned on me: strange and bizarre things had happened to me my whole life. I never thought it was me, but maybe it was. I felt relieved knowing that an evil spirit hadn't been haunting me my whole life. As I walked along the dark roadside, I thought about each event and how Aku might be right. I must be a mage!

It was really dark out now, and I was getting a little scared. The streetlights came on, but it didn't stop the darkness. Thoughts of how and where I had drawn the negative attention kept crossing my mind. Maybe mentioning my real last name had started it? I was still confused though. Being put up for adoption from a family of sorcerers made no sense. How could powerful sorcerers give up their only child? I wanted to know more.

Arriving home extremely late, I saw Mom sitting in her chair through the window. I was never home this late, and I knew she was going to be mad, but I couldn't tell her where I really was. When I walked in, she jumped up from her chair and started yelling at me.

"Where have you been?" she cried. "I was about to call the police! Ms. Maggie told me you left early this morning and never came back."

"I finally made a friend today, at the park," I said, trying to make up a story on the spot. "I lost track of time and didn't realize how late it was until I saw it was getting dark."

"I was worried sick, Anya," she said, calming down.

"I'm sixteen now," I said abruptly. "I need more freedom."

"I knew this was coming," she said with a sigh and a sad look on her face. "We will work on some new rules."

"I'm sorry for scaring you," I said. "I won't do it again."

I was tired from all the walking and was ready to go to bed. Mom had left dinner on the stove for me. I made myself a small plate of mac and cheese with a hotdog before heading upstairs. I laid in bed for hours, and of course I couldn't sleep. I kept thinking about these powers that I had. I set up a bunch of books to test myself. Part of me still didn't believe it, but another part of me thought, *what if, what if I really could move things with my mind?* Still in disbelief, I laughed and tried to focus. *Come on, book, move already.* I could feel the veins in my head strain as I tried. Nothing! Nothing was happening.

I was getting so mad, and that's when, suddenly, a book lifted up! It lifted off the desk then dropped on the floor. Actually, it more like slammed on the floor.

"Is everything ok?" Mom yelled from her room.

I quickly jumped into bed and turned off the lamp. I heard her footsteps coming. She opened my door and turned on the light

"I heard a thump and thought you fell out of bed," she said.

"I threw some clothes off my bed, and they hit my nightstand," I replied. "They must have knocked the books over."

"You're so clumsy, Anya," she laughed. "Get some sleep. It's getting late."

Yeah, that'll be easy. If only I could tell my brain to go to sleep. My mind kept racing. What else could I do? How was I going to use my powers? Who could I tell about this? What dangers was I going to face?

4

NOWHERE TO HIDE

I woke up the next day and couldn't smell anything coming from the kitchen. I thought it was odd. Mom always had something ready for me before she left for work. I crept downstairs to see what was going on. No Mom or breakfast, just a note she left for me on the table.

Sorry, Hun, was running late this morning. There are some breakfast sandwiches in the freezer. Love you, Mom.

Well, that had never happened before.

I went over to the freezer and opened it up. I was disappointed to see a croissant, egg, and sausage sandwich. I didn't normally eat microwaved food because it had a strange aftertaste. I put it in the microwave anyways and waited for it to finish. I took my first bite, but the meat was like rubber. I couldn't eat it. I had to throw it away. Disappointed, I grabbed a banana and went back upstairs to get changed. I decided I was going to go back to the library today and do some research on Asa and Amoura Vamour. I knew Aku said not to, but I knew their names now, and I was sure Google would know something.

It was a beautiful day out as I began my walk down the drive towards town. I could hear birds chirping and watch as the clouds crossed the sky. I began to daydream, and I tried to imagine the clouds as different animals. I was almost to the library when I saw Aku. He hadn't seen me, so I waved hello. He stopped me.

"DO NOT go to the library today," he said. I questioned him, but he seemed anxious about something.

"Go home and stay there," he said. "I'll meet you there later."

I didn't understand what was going on. I just stood there confused as I watched him look around and then walk away. I began to follow him, but he stopped and looked at me.

"It's time to go," he whispered. "You are no longer safe here."

"Safe from what?" I whispered back. I could see he was getting frustrated with me.

"There's no time to explain." He began to walk down the street towards my home now. I kept following him, looking back towards town. I didn't see anything out of the ordinary. Nothing seemed to be following us. Maybe he really was crazy.

When we got back to the house, I turned to Aku. "Safe from what?" I asked again.

"They found you," he said, looking at me.

"Who are they?"

"Wereman. The demons I told you about. The ones who seek out sorcerers. I think they're the same ones who took your parents."

Aku kept pacing back and forth and checking all the windows. He closed the blinds and said to stay away from the doors and windows. I started to feel a little disturbed, but I knew Mom would eventually get home. After several hours of watching Aku pace around the house, I finally heard Mom pulling into the driveway. Aku jumped up.

"Stay away from the windows!" he shouted.

"It must be my mom," I said, looking at him.

He peeked through the blinds and appeared to relax. As she opened the door, I knew I was going to have to explain why there was a man in the house.

"MOM!" I cried. "I'm ok, but my friend Aku is here."

She was excited to meet my new friend until she saw a grown man. She yelled at him for hanging out with little girls and started to call the police. I grabbed the phone and hung it up as I told her the truth. Aku was the one that told me all about my parents. She still didn't seem to trust him. I pulled over a chair, and I told her to just wait and watch what I could do. I focused really hard and suddenly the chair tipped over. I could see she was confused and a little startled.

"I was scared at first too, Mom," I said. "Do you remember the books I knocked over last night? It wasn't by accident."

After she calmed down some, she started talking to Aku, asking what all this meant for me. I could tell Mom was getting really upset again, so I went to my room. Later Aku came upstairs to talk.

"Your mom understands now," he said. "We need to go somewhere safe."

"I'm perfectly safe with Mom," I replied.

"The same bad things that found your parents have found you too. You're no longer safe here in your town or in your home."

Wereman and magic—this was all just too much to take in. I stormed out of my room and sat on the top of the steps looking downstairs, wondering what I had done. How were we going to get past this? I could hear Aku making phone calls from my room and Mom crying from the kitchen. I knew this was not going to be good. It hurt to hear her crying. I had never heard her cry like that before. She probably felt like she was losing me, but we were a team, and she would just go with me if I had to leave. After Aku finished his calls, he came out from my room and sat with me.

"Is my mom coming with us?" I asked him.

"I have to talk with her," he said. "But it looks like we have the night to decide. My people won't be here until morning.

"I'm not going anywhere without her," I said.

He got up and walked downstairs to the kitchen. I could hear them talking, but it was like whispers from the top of the stairs. She wouldn't just let me go like this. All I could think of was, what in the world was really going on? Was this a dream? Was I going to wake up soon? When they came from the kitchen, Mom looked up at me.

"We're going in the morning," she said.

"Where?" I asked.

"I'm not sure, honey," she said, looking at Aku.

As things began to settle down for the night, I tried to get some sleep. As I lay in bed, I started to hear things from outside my window. Not people talking or animals rustling in the woods, but a clanking sound. I looked outside and saw something dash in the moonlight. I freaked out, screaming, and went to run but tripped, making a loud thud. Aku ran to me as I made it to the bottom of the stairs.

"Is everything ok?" he asked.

Before I could say anything, Mom came running in from the kitchen.

"There's something outside!" she shouted. Aku looked around before asking Mom if there was a basement, but we didn't have one. He quickly started to look around for something. He started to pull open some wood panels on our wall that we were fixing behind the stairs.

"Both of you, get in and be quiet," he said.

We squeezed in, and he put the panel over us.

As soon as Aku was able to hide, the front door flung open. All I could see from the narrow gap in the wall was a shadow. Whatever it was, it was large enough to bust through the front door. We could hear footsteps as it went in and out of different rooms. It was breathing very heavily, and things were being tossed everywhere. That was when I really saw it. It was shaped like a man, but maybe three times larger than a normal man. It had no neck and a small head when compared to its body. Its breathing was all I could hear. Aku busted out from the hall closet and pinned the thing down on the ground. Whatever it was let out a loud shrieking noise.

"Run to the barn!" Aku yelled.

We slid out from behind the wall, and Mom grabbed my hand as we took off running, out of the house and across the yard to the barn. Once we made it inside, we pulled the doors shut, locking them. We turned around to look for something to block the door when another man came up behind us. We both shrieked.

"It's ok! I'm a friend of your uncle," he said. "I'm here to help, but we need to go now."

"What about him?" I cried. "We can't leave him!"

"He'll be fine, he can handle himself," the man said.

"Anya, we've got to go, we've got to go now," Mom said. We fled the barn, piling into the man's black Suburban. We drove through town and kept going.

"Where are we going?" Mom asked.

"I'm taking Anya to a safe house," he said.

"I'm going with her!" Mom cried. He didn't respond.

"My mom is coming with me!" I said. He just nodded.

We pulled up to a private runway, hidden between hayfields in the middle of nowhere. He drove through the field and stopped next to a small jet waiting on the track before getting out. It was dark outside, and the moonlight was all we had to see with. There were some lights on inside the small plane, and when the door was opened, lights lit up the stairs. As we were getting ready to board, my uncle drove up in a small car. He was covered in dirt and wet from something. I got in the plane while Mom was talking with him. I waited a few minutes, but Mom never got on. I got up to see what was taking so long and made it to the door when I saw my uncle holding my mom back. He had his arms around her waist, holding her from behind as she kicked and screamed for me. He was dragging her back to the dark Suburban.

"What the hell are you doing?" I yelled, panicking. The man who drove us started walking towards me up the steps into the plane.

"She can't go with us, those are the orders," he said, blocking my path off the plane. I went to push him out of the way, but someone from behind grabbed me. I was dragged to my seat and held like a prisoner.

"Only you can go," the man grabbing me explained. "Your uncle will take care of your mom until you can see her again." I began to panic and hyperventilate as I leaned over, trying to capture my breath. My chest hurt as I struggled to take in air and calm myself. I could see the lights turn on along the runway as the plane turned on its loud engine. My uncle was pushing my mom back into the vehicle. I tried kicking the man holding me back as I tried to scream between breathes until the plane left the ground.

As the plane flew farther into the night sky, I couldn't stop worrying about Mom. What if that creature found her? Who was going to protect her? What was Aku doing? All of these questions left an unsettling feeling in my stomach. I felt alone and afraid. I didn't know these people or where they were taking me. The more I wondered about where I might end up, the more worried I became. I sat in silence for a couple of hours wondering what lay ahead. I tried so hard to keep from crying. I just kept looking out into the dark sky with tears running down my cheeks.

The man that drove us to the plane came over and sat near me.

"My name is Derek," he said. "If you need anything just call me. There's nothing to be afraid of. Aku sent me to take you to a safe place. You'll do well there, learning more about your gifts."

I couldn't hold my tears back and kept crying. We talked for about an hour before he finally told me we were headed to New Zealand. I began to panic.

"We can't leave the country," I said, crying.

"This is going to be a new home for you to grow up in," he said.

I wondered when I would see Mom again. He moved a few rows closer to the cockpit as I looked out the window and continued to cry. I wished I had never started looking for my parents.

5
REFUGEE

Five hours had passed, and time felt as if it had slowed down. Derek had stood up and come back to my seat, sitting next to me. I was half asleep and not in the mood to talk.

"The man you will be staying with is called Seth. He is very familiar with your biological parents and the situation you're in," he said with a smile on his face. "He's a little strange at first, but you'll get used to his personality quickly," Derek explained. "You should listen to everything he says. Seth knows so much that you will need to learn before you can face your demons."

"What does that mean, face my demons?" I questioned.

"Seth will explain in time."

As the plane neared what looked like a mansion up on a cliff landing, I couldn't help but wonder if that was where we were going. There was nothing but woods and high mountains all around. Derek looked at me.

"We're here," he said. I was nervous to meet Seth, but if he knew my parents, maybe he could help me find them. I looked out the window, staring at the huge mansion. As the plane prepared to land, I could see the trees around the mansion with a wide-open view of the cliff in the back. It was still dark out—it was maybe two or three in the morning—but there were plenty of lights that lined the private air strip and walkways around the courtyard. Lights were on in quite a few rooms as well. There was a beautiful fountain out front I could see glowing as we circled around back. I was excited that this was where I would be staying but nervous at the same time. I wished Mom could have been here to see this. She would have loved it.

We circled again before coming up to the landing strip along the side of the home. As the plane landed, all I could think about was how big this place was. This couldn't just be for one person. When the plane came to a stop and the door opened, Derek led me out.

"Just go in through the front door," he said. "Someone will meet you there."

I was confused that he wasn't coming with me, especially since he brought me all this way. *What if I just ran off?* I looked around to see my options. I was a ways away from the nearest wood line and remembered that there was nothing but woods and mountains all around me.

I began walking towards the giant entrance as the wind blew my hair into my face. I kept needing to flip my hair back as I watched the plane take off. I was alone in the dark, chilly night, walking up to a stranger's home. I followed the lit cobblestone pathway. It appeared whitewashed or maybe just old. Walking along, I thought about their security system and hoped they didn't have any dogs or alarm systems. I made it safely to another path that led away from the landing strip going to the driveway.

As I got closer, I was amazed at how tall the home was. I had been walking along a side that was two stories tall but as I came around, some parts of the building looked like they were four or five stories. I made my way to the paved driveway and could finally see the incredible fountain I had seen from the plane. It was in the center of the driveway, with a glowing blue light that cascaded over the driveway. At the center of the fountain was a statue of a woman with a spout coming from the palm of her hand. As I turned towards the front entrance, I stopped and looked at how enormous it was before taking a few deep breaths. There were large pillars on both sides of the walkway leading up to the doors, a few steps to the first landing, and a few more before reaching the front door.

Should I knock? Or just go in? What should I say if someone answered the door? As I was about to knock, the door suddenly opened. I was startled by the doorman.

"Hello Anya, I am Roger the butler. Come in, and I'll show you to your room," he said cheerfully. I looked in the doorway at the marble checkered flooring and warm, inviting artwork of animals hung throughout. The entryway seemed like a large circular area with paths leading to different parts of the home.

"Thank you," I said hesitantly, as I followed him down a very long hallway. It was a tall, narrow hallway with more nature paintings, but these were of cranes and storks hung very high up. Near the end of the hall, we slowed down, and I noticed a beautiful pastel painting of a flamingo that had vibrant blue water painted below it and a beautiful orange horizon behind it. Roger stopped in front of a room before he turned to me.

"There should be a note for you from Seth on the dresser," he said. "I hope you find everything you will need in here, and if there is anything I can get for you, please just ask."

I was so intrigued by the note, I scanned the room quickly and went straight in to grab it from the top of the dresser. The note read:

Dear Anya:

Sorry I was not there to greet you myself, but I had important matters to attend to. I know that your arrival is very late, and I am sure you are tired. I will have a car arranged to drive you to "The Secret Clubhouse" where we can meet and go over a few brief house rules. I will arrange for three, but if you are not at the house by then, Roger will let me know.

See you soon,

Seth

I wondered about the secret clubhouse. It sounded mysteriously exciting and a little childish. I had never been invited to a clubhouse before. How old was Seth that he still had a clubhouse? I had some time to kill before I had to meet Seth, which only made me more anxious. I put the note down and looked around my new room. I was taking it all in when I noticed the drawers were full of clothes already, the bed was beautifully made, and the windows had curtains that hung from the ceilings. I went over to look out the window and noticed there were bars on the outside of all the windows.

The room was painted a cream white, and there were more nature paintings hanging on the walls. The room was a decent size and held a dresser, desk, bed, and a wardrobe. I opened the wardrobe and was excited to see a backpack hanging inside. I loved my travel pack I left back home, but this one was new. I pulled it off the hook and tried it on. It was blue, my favorite color. It fit great, and I hung it back up with hopes to use it soon. I went to sit on the bed, and as I did, I noticed dirt falling off me onto the bed. I hurried to brush the dirt from the bright yellow duvet before anyone noticed I messed it up. I needed a shower desperately. I grabbed some clothes that appeared to fit from one of the drawers and went to find a shower.

I got a little lost in the maze of a home trying to find the bathroom and eventually ran into the nice doorman again.

"Hey, Roger, sorry to bother you, but I seem to be a bit lost trying to find the bathroom?" I clenched my change of clothes in my arms.

"No bother at all, Ms. Anya," he said pleasantly. "I told you if you ever needed anything just ask."

He led me to the bathroom and showed me how to turn on the shower. It was the most complicated thing I had ever seen. I had to turn the shower on with one knob, pull down the lever to get hot water, adjust the water temp with another lever, and then pull out another knob for the water to come down from above.

The bathroom was surprisingly smaller than I would have imagined for such a large place. It had the same checkered flooring that was in the entryway but in much smaller pieces. There was a pedestal sink to my left when I first walked in, and a toilet tucked behind a wall across from the sink. The bath was straight in against the back wall. After finally getting into the shower, it felt so wonderful, I didn't want to get out. It was getting close to three, though, and I had to get ready to meet Seth.

After I got cleaned up and dressed in the new clothes, I went to find Roger once again.

"I need to meet with Seth, but I'm not sure how to get to the secret clubhouse he mentioned in his note," I said, once I found him.

"A driver will pick you up and take you there," he replied.

"What's the clubhouse?" I asked, while I waited.

"It's a restaurant for sorcerers to get together safely," Roger answered. "Seth actually owns it."

"I thought it was like a secret fort," I laughed.

"It's much better than a fort," he chuckled.

The driver pulled up in a black limo and opened the back door for me to get in. I looked back at Roger and waved goodbye.

"It was a pleasure talking with you, Ms. Anya," Roger said. *He was a really nice old man,* I thought to myself. I wondered if he had powers like me and wished I had asked him.

It took about ten minutes through winding, dark roads before we arrived at the Clubhouse. As we pulled into the parking lot, it looked like a normal restaurant, with lights on and music playing. There were plenty of vehicles parked outside, and I could hear people laughing and talking on the patio.

As the driver pulled around and let me out, I began to get nervous and could feel my palms getting sweaty. I walked inside and looked around the crowded room. Not sure of what Seth looked like, I wandered around the restaurant for a few minutes. I didn't want to just shout out his name. There was a man all by himself in a corner booth on the far side of the room. I thought he might be Seth, but I wasn't sure. Then the man saw me.

"Anya, glad you made it!" he yelled out while waving me over. "Please, please sit down." As I sat, a waitress quickly came over to take our order. I requested pop while Seth ordered a beer.

"Do you want a starter? Maybe some fries?" he asked kindly.

"Ugh, no, thank you. I'm not really hungry" I said. My nerves made me more nauseous than hungry. Our waitress soon walked off to get our drinks.

"Do you like my home so far?" he asked. "How do you feel about staying with me for a while?"

"I'd be happier if you had let my mother come," I told him, anger in my voice. He looked at me with shock.

"Your mother isn't like you. She wouldn't be safe with us," he said. "You will have full protection all the time, which is why Aku sent you here to begin with. There are other people living there that are just like you, and you'll fit in just fine. We're like one big family. There are four others, all with different gifts, that came seeking protection, like you are doing tonight."

"We all look out for each other and learn from one another," he said sternly. "Oh, and there is only one rule you have to follow: no sorcery in the house!"

None of this mattered to me. All I could think about was Mom and how sad she must be.

"I want to know when I can see my mom again," I asked hesitantly.

"You'll see her as soon as things settle down," he assured me. "You can see her when you can protect yourself."

The more we talked, the more I felt like I could trust him. However, he wouldn't tell me what he did or what his powers were. I didn't understand why but thought maybe in time he would tell me, so I left it alone for the night. We wrapped up our conversation, and he walked me outside, where his driver was waiting patiently to take me back to the house.

"Goodnight," he said, opening the door to let me into the car. I was surprised he wasn't going back with me, since the sky was lightening and the sun would be coming up soon.

"Are you coming?" I asked. He shook his head.

"There is work to be done."

He shut the door and waved me off as I sat there surprised by his words. What work needed to be done this early in the morning?

6

THE REUNION

Weeks went by, and I hadn't been able to see or hear from my mom. I felt a bit lonely at times. It had been a little over three months since my birthday, when all this began. I still hadn't met everyone who lived in the mansion yet. It was empty most of the time. I met Jane, who was seventeen, thin, and pretty, with long red hair and hazel eyes. She was a huge partier and loved to go to The Clubhouse late at night. She seemed nice but was a little odd at times. I never knew which side of her I was going to get—Nice Jane or Wild Jane. She was a loner like me, yet she loved attention at times.

I will never forget the first morning I was there and she scared me half to death. I woke up around noon and wandered the halls in search of the kitchen. As I walked through a hall with a wall of pillars, Jane jumped out from behind one of them, sword drawn.

Towering over me she shouted, "Get on the ground!"

I dropped to my knees with my hands raised in the air before hearing her bust out laughing. I thought I was going to pee myself. "Why the hell would you do that?" I screamed "You nearly gave me a heart attack!"

She continued to laugh so hard she was bent over nearly on the floor. "I'm sorry, I'm not used to people being scared so easily. I'm Jane."

After that, we became fast friends. We didn't have much in common, but it was nice to have someone to talk to. When we went to The Clubhouse on Friday nights, she treated me like an annoying little sister. I thought of it as her way of trying to impress the guys there. And I'd never had a sister, so I didn't mind.

As the weeks went by, we grew closer to one another. On one of our many walks, I asked about the others that have yet to come home.

"There are three others that stay here at the mansion, but they have been away for a while. They are on some important mission that I wasn't allowed to go on," she said aggressively.

"Who are these three others?"

"Eddy, Zane, and Rosswick. All guys, which makes it hard for me to hang out with them all the time. They act stupid and immature when they're all together."

"Do they have powers like me?" I asked. "Hey! I never asked you, what can you do?"

"Yes, in fact, Zane is a mage like you," she said. "Rosswick is some sort of healer, and Eddy is a mutant with super strength."

"What's your special ability?" I asked again.

"I guess we'll never know," she said before running off.

I wondered what the big secret was. Maybe she was embarrassed about it.

My schedule eventually became more hectic. One cold morning Seth came to my room early and said it was time to begin training. I wondered what I would be training on—potions, spells, maybe curses? I still was not familiar with what I was or what I could do.

"Can I eat breakfast first?" I asked, still half asleep.

"Yes, I have to run out for a bit, but meet me in the courtyard at ten, which should give you a couple hours to wake up," he said, chuckling on his way out.

I staggered out of bed and eventually made myself some cereal before sitting on the couch with a hot cup of tea. Staring out the window, all I could think was that it was too early to be functioning. It was nearly ten when Jane came staggering through the living area across from the kitchen. She plopped herself down on the couch and looked at me with confusion.

"Good morning sunshine, not used to seeing you up this early," she said in her loud, high-pitched voice.

"Seth wants to train this morning. If you don't be quiet, I will use whatever spell I learn today on you," I said, still tired and cranky.

"Seth doesn't teach you spells right out the gate. You're going to learn combat!" she said excitedly.

"Combat? Why would I learn that if I could just use my gift on someone?"

"He teaches everyone combat," she said with a delighted smile on her face.

I looked down into my cup. "Nope this is not going to do it. I'm gonna need coffee."

I got up and made myself coffee before heading to the courtyard. I sat down in the corner and took my first sip of coffee just as Seth walked in.

"What are you doing? You should be stretching," he said as he walked up to me.

After stretches, Seth asked if I favored any sort of weapons.

"Weapons? No, I've never used a weapon before. Maybe a pocketknife when I hike, but I never needed to use it," I said.

He dragged a rolling wall from the attached shed in the back that was covered with many different kinds of swords and daggers hanging from pegs. My jaw nearly dropped when he pushed it out. *He's trying to kill me,* I thought to myself.

"Come try some out and pick what feels comfortable to you," Seth said. Surprised, I walked over to the wall and picked the longest sword on it. I could barely hold it up.

"Maybe one that you can handle," he said.

I laughed as I struggled to put it back in its holder. I picked up two small daggers, but they felt strange to hold.

"I don't want to get this close to someone if I have to fight with blades," I said, unsure.

"Well, if it doesn't feel right, try another."

My eyes were drawn to a sword not nearly as long as the first one I had tried. It had an interesting curve to its blade. I drew it from the wall and held it in my hand. It felt comfortable enough for me to grip and not too heavy for me to wield.

"This is the one. I like this one!" I said in excitement.

"Great choice. That's a katana. I think it will be a good fit for you."

Our first day of training consisted of mostly Seth teaching me how to hold and wield my blade. In the days that followed, I learned more and more techniques. I trained in sword fighting with Seth on Mondays and Thursdays, and eventually sorcery mastering on Tuesdays and Fridays. Seth got me schoolwork to do on my down time, but I could do that work whenever I wanted, like when I was homeschooling with Mom.

Sorcery training was not what I was expecting. I figured I would just be learning how to use my powers rather than control them. I quickly discovered I reacted through my emotions and needed to learn another way. Seth challenged me physically and psychologically so I would react appropriately and learn other ways to handle threats. He taught me how to control my impulses instead of reacting with erratic, emotion-driven powers. During a random field training session, Seth set up some surprise manikins to see how I would react. I initially destroyed my housemate imitation manikins until I learned to look first and react accordingly to actual danger or just surprises. I also continued to learn the strength of concentration so that I could move objects around, like I had at home. After all the training, I hadn't learned any other spells during those first few months at the mansion.

It was hard to talk to Seth other than when we were training. He was constantly away and hard to reach. Our training sessions were usually an hour long, so I never had a lot of time to talk to him. He would always take off after receiving a phone call, which got annoying after a while. I wondered what he was doing, but I never could ask him.

I spent the rest of my time reading in my room or walking around and exploring with Jane. I wanted to check out the surrounding woods, but she acted as if we weren't supposed to go into the woods. Instead, we would usually walk the perimeter of the property. During another one of our walks, I told her I was getting tired of doing the same things all the time.

"What do you mean?" she asked.

"I don't know, I just feel like I'm wasting my gift and that there is more out there I need to be doing with it," I said, disappointed in myself.

"That's normal. Zane said he went through the same thing. Eventually Seth will let you go on missions and that feeling will go away," she said supportively.

"Missions? Why would I go on missions?" I asked, confused.

"Everyone goes on missions. It's you doing your part to stay here."

"I guess I just don't understand where or why you're sent on a mission," I said.

"You'll see eventually. I'm sure the guys will be back soon, and they will tell you all about their exciting adventure," Jane reassured me. "Seth selects what missions you go on based on what the mission is and what your skill sets are. Sometimes we all have to go, and sometimes just one of us has to go."

Weeks later, during one of my lessons with Seth, he informed me that there was going to be a house meeting. There hadn't been one in a while, but the guys were finally getting back from their mission. I would finally get the chance to meet the rest of the family.

"When is the meeting going to be?" I asked, trying to hold back my excitement.

"Friday, at eight in the evening. The boys should be back by then," Seth replied.

"So tomorrow?" I asked, wondering if he meant next week.

"Yes, tomorrow, Anya. We will meet in the conservatory," he said with a smile.

Friday came quickly, and I rushed to get to the conservatory early. I didn't usually spend much time in there, but it was very relaxing. It was an extension to the mansion off the back side made mostly of glass panes. There was a large fireplace on one side and lots of cactuses and air plants. There was seating all the way around, but I sat near the fireplace to keep warm. The floor had the same black and white checkered tile as a lot of places inside the home. I didn't care much for it.

The meeting was supposed to start at eight, but only Jane, Seth, and I were on time. Seth spent the time waiting on his phone, glancing up every now and again.

"So where are the guys?" Jane finally asked. Seth lowered his phone.

"They're running a bit late but should be here soon!" he said, annoyed. We continued to sit, awkwardly and quietly waiting for them to arrive.

Finally, around nine thirty, the guys arrived. I remained quiet in my corner near the fireplace. We could hear them coming, laughing loudly, before we saw them entering the room. They were shoving each other and still laughing about something. As I looked at the three of them, I was instantly drawn to one in particular: a tall, slender man with thick hair and a mysterious bad boy look. He had a long, intense jawline and a lean body. He wore torn blue jeans and a dark leather jacket.

I must have been staring quite a while, because he eventually looked over at me, and before I knew it, my heart began to race. He then smiled at me before Seth hugged him. I felt flustered, with butterflies in my stomach. I had never felt this way before. I could see Seth talking with him before they both started to walk towards me. My heart beating rapidly, I tried to swallow the saliva in my mouth before they arrived.

"Anya, this is Zane," Seth said. "He is also a katana wielder like you." *What are the odds that he chose the katana too?* I thought to myself.

"Cool, maybe we could duel sometime?" I asked hesitantly, looking up at Zane. He towered over me. I hadn't realized how much taller he was than I. Zane stared back at me and nodded. He looked like he was only a couple years older than me.

"Zane can help you understand your special abilities and control them better, since he is also a mage," Seth continued. "Zane is the best sorcerer in the house."

"Sure, I can help her," Zane said, looking at me with a smile.

I was frozen and barely able to utter the word. "Thanks," I finally muttered. I wasn't sure if it was his cute smile or his soft stare, but I couldn't wait till we could see each other again. Seth seemed pleased.

"Let's get this meeting started, shall we?" Seth said, as he led us to our seats.

When the meeting finally began, Seth stood in front of all of us and asked for Eddy to come up. I wasn't sure which one was Eddy until he launched himself up from his seat. He stood there a moment taking off his jacket, flashing his incredible muscles that were rippling through his shirt. He was much shorter than Zane. I wondered if we were the same height. He confidently marched over to Seth, and they stood next to each other as Seth began his speech.

"Welcome back from another successful mission everyone!" Seth said. "I hate to say welcome back and then tell you that there is another mission, but unfortunately that's what there is. Eddy here needs our help retrieving a few items that were stolen from him while he and the guys were away. We are all aware of Eddy's so-called safe house he built."

"Maybe not the new girl," Eddy interrupted, with a demeaning tone.

"Anya, it was a cabin Eddy built nearly five miles from the mansion because he felt his most precious items were not safe here," Seth said sarcastically. "While the guys were away, unbeknown to me, the cabin was raided before it was set ablaze. The items that were taken are important relics to his people and their realm."

I nodded as everyone stared at me.

"In a few short months, when everyone is more prepared, you are all going to go on this mission to help Eddy," Seth said. "It won't be too dangerous—an easy mission for a first timer. Eddy will be gathering all the information he needs to locate his items while the rest of you should be preparing."

"I will update everyone if there are any special circumstances we should know before we leave," Eddy quickly added.

"Keep up the good work, everyone, and continue to respect one another," Seth concluded.

Seth turned away from us to speak to Eddy. Everyone else started talking about what the mystery mission for Eddy really was about.

"Mystery mission? I thought we were helping him find his stolen items?" I interrupted everyone.

"The missions are never what they appear to be," Jane replied before turning back to the guys. I sat back and pondered what that was supposed to mean. I overheard Seth talking to Eddy.

"Retrieving your items is all you're gonna to focus on with Anya. Make sure she's safe!" Seth said quietly to Eddy. "And make sure Jane does what she needs to do."

"We can't keep doing this Seth. Do you realize how hard it is on these missions to get away from the guys?" Eddy replied.

"You know we do the things we do so we can live the way we live."

Eddy began to respond, but he seemed to get quieter while the others seemed to get louder. I kept my eyes on the others but continued to try and listen to Seth and Eddy. Unable to hear anymore, I wondered what they were talking about. It seemed like Jane was right— these missions weren't ordinary trips.

Later, I was properly introduced to the other two guys, Rosswick and Eddy. I already knew from Jane that Rosswick's special ability was healing. I walked over to him.

"Hey, I'm Anya," I said. Rosswick seemed surprised by my abruptness.

"Nice to meet you, Anya. I'm Rosswick. If you ever need anything, let me know," he said politely before walking away. He was tall like Zane, but a little thicker. His hair was short, light brown almost blond. His eyes were a soft hazel color with a pop of yellow in them. He appeared to be older than Zane, maybe in his mid-twenties. He had carried a couple books around with him all night and glanced through them at times. I didn't ask him about it, but he had to be very smart since the books he had were about botany and astronomy.

Eddy's gift, on the other hand, was obviously super strength. I remembered Jane said he was a mutant. As I walked past him, I wanted to introduce myself.

"Hey," I said when he looked my way. He ignored me, flexing his muscles on one arm and telling Rosswick to touch it. He seemed arrogant and full of himself as he spent the evening bench pressing Jane with one arm then tossing her to the other like it was nothing.

Jane seemed to adore Eddy as she gawked at him most of the night. I don't know why she liked him so much—he was a short guy that seemed rude, but he did have a lot of muscles. He looked like he was in his late teens or maybe early twenties. He had black hair and dark brown eyes that made him seem distrusting. I didn't care much for him as the night progressed. He would talk over everyone and kept turning every story around to talk about himself.

Before the evening finally ended, Zane came over to me to talk.

"How skilled are you with your sorcery?" he asked.

"I'm not great. Seth seemed to teach me more control than anything else," I said. "But he has shown me a few levitational spells so far." Zane shook his head, looking disappointed.

"Have you been studying in the library?" he asked with a serious look on his face.

"I didn't even know we had one," I said, laughing. He didn't find it amusing though.

"Maybe you should be spending your free time there, instead of running around with Jane," he responded.

"I haven't been running around with Jane," I said defensively.

"That's what I've heard from The Clubhouse." He smirked at me.

I stood there, unsure of what to say. He laughed and put his arm on my shoulder. "I'm just messing with you, but seriously check out the library. It will help your sorcery and you'll learn about other cultures. Goodnight!" he said before leaving the conservatory.

7

LEARNING IN THE LIBRARY

I tried to focus on training and preparing myself for our upcoming mission. The more I thought about it, the more nervous it made me. What were we really going to do on this mission? I wanted to know what Seth had Jane and Eddy doing. I wondered why Seth kept that secret from Zane and Rosswick and only shared it with Jane and Eddy. So many questions had crossed my mind since our meeting.

Zane started to work with me on Tuesdays and Fridays with extra magic training.

"Have you been reading in the library like I told you?" he asked, nearly a week after our meeting with Seth. Stunned by the unexpected question, I slowly and disappointedly shook my head.

"No, but I promise I will start tonight."

He acted annoyed as he shuffled through the healing petals laid across the table. I wondered if we were going to learn which petals would save my life or kill me. I stood there awkwardly, waiting for him to respond or turn around.

"I tell you to do these things because they will help you understand," he muttered as I stared at his back, disappointed in myself. I wondered what was so special about this library that I had to go read these books.

That is, until I discovered the library and the mysteries of the world it held inside. The library was on the far side of the mansion, not too far from the conservatory. I enlisted some help from Roger to show me after not being able to find it myself. It was a massive room with tons of books. I wasn't sure how I ever missed it. The room was enormous and well-lit, with bookcases all along the back wall. There were a few chairs around the room and a large round red rug in the center. I browsed through some cases and quickly learned these books weren't just ordinary books. There were texts on everything from realms and demons to spells and curses. I instantly found myself lost among the pages and made myself a pile of books on the carpet.

I started out researching mages, trying to figure out what exactly I was. I opened the first book to the first chapter:

Mages are sorcerers with the ability to cast spells and harness unique powers. There are different levels of mages. Those at the highest level are called archmages, a birthright passed from the purest line to chosen mages. They have the ability to master all forms of spells and rule over realms. Black mages practice the art of offensive magic. Summoners are those who call upon beasts or deities.

I was so fascinated, I couldn't stop, and the more I read the more fascinated I became.

For the next several nights, I went back to the library to find myself lost in books about the different realms. The real world only knew about what they could see, but the realms were different worlds inside the real world.

Only those with gifts can find and access realm gateways, usually with keys or maps. Some have access to portal doors, which are secret ways to enter different realms without traveling to the location of the gateway.

It was so exciting to discover there were all of these places that no one in the real world knew about. I thought about Mom, and what she would say. She would probably freak out if she knew any of this. The next chapter I began to read was about gatekeepers.

Realms are accessed by gateways and there are chosen beings for each realm called gatekeepers. Whenever there is an issue, whether in the realm or outside of it, they are summoned to maintain that realm. The realms themselves choose who their next gatekeeper will be after the last one passes. If no one is selected, then the realm places a gate key somewhere hidden inside a realm object, usually a book or map. This is used as an emergency access in case something goes wrong within the realm.

Months of hard training and dueling had followed since our meeting. Seth had focused on my katana wielding since Zane was focusing more on my abilities. Seth would spend hours teaching me hand-to-hand combat and agility training aside from dueling. He would often set up obstacle courses to trick me into battle scenes or unexpected dueling while trying to get out of tough spots he created.

I missed my mom more and more each day. It was now almost my seventeenth birthday, and I would hate for Mom to miss it. I often asked Seth if I could call her or write letters. Seth never gave me much hope, though.

"In time," he would say. This infuriated me and I reacted in anger. I would go days with minimal conversations with him or I would shout at him.

"Maybe if you'd let me talk to my mom I'd do better," I'd yell when I would fail at a task during training. I felt it was never going to be time, and it made me frustrated.

I found myself returning to the library often, and each time I came I learned about something new and exciting. I discovered some spell books and quickly took to them. I came across one called *Stimot*. This was a spell that enabled a mage to inhabit another living being. The mage would then see what the other being saw and hear what they heard. This reminded me of what happened to me and the dingo back home. I couldn't help but remain fascinated with every page I turned to. *Zumada* was the next spell I read about, which gave the caster super speed. *Ackura* was the spell for light. I found another spell for levitation called *Levotia*. I was glad I brought a notebook. I made a ton of notes to practice some of the spells with Zane. There were so many others, I just wouldn't remember them all unless I looked at my notebook. I wondered how great sorcerers remembered all of these.

I spent my seventeenth birthday on the floor of the library reading about demon wolves and their subspecies. I didn't want to tell anyone that it was my birthday because it felt wrong without my mom there. Zane had encouraged me at our last class to read about demons and other beasts from the many realms. I spent hours scouring books on the many creatures I may encounter one day and the realms they lived in. I read:

Demon wolves live to protect the secret of the realms and act as judges when rules have been broken, even though they aren't realm keepers. They act more like unlawful justice seekers. They interfere when they believe realm keepers aren't protecting the secrets of their realms.

The realm of demon wolves is called Valdekka. They exist in four divided colonies. The hierarchy starts at the top tier, a group called shifters. They are capable of changing from human to wolf and back again. Youngsters usually need a mask. Often made from past relatives in their wolf form, this aids their transformation until they master their abilities. Next are super wolves. Once they reach an age of maturity they evolve into an oversized wolf. Usually adolescent at age of transformation, they are unable to change back into human form. Next are werewolves, a cross between human and wolf. They walk on two legs, are covered in fur, and stand nearly nine feet in height. Lastly are wereman. They are the black sheep of their kind, a mutt made when a female shifter mates with a male werewolf. They walk on all four legs and can reach heights up to six feet tall while on all fours. They act as a wolf but appear as a human with patches of fur and overextended limbs.

Nearing the end of the chapter on demon wolves, I heard someone coming. It was late at night, and I didn't think anyone was still awake. I quietly put the books from my lap onto the floor as I stared intensely at the doorway. To my surprise, it was Zane.

"Hey," he said as I jumped in fright. "Didn't mean to startle you."

"What are you doing? Besides giving me a heart attack," I managed to get out as I calmed down.

"I just wanted to see how your studies were going and if you had any questions." He sat down on the floor next to me.

"It's fine," I said before pausing for a moment. "Where are we going on this mission?" I asked.

"We are going to a realm called Hardgate, It's actually where Rosswick is from," Zane said in a reassuring tone. "Why did you want to know"

"I don't know, just curious of what to expect there," I said.

"I wouldn't worry. It's a peaceful place where refugees usually coexist quite well together," he assured me. "Anything else bothering you?"

"Well, I keep wondering why demon wolves would take my parents."

"Many changes have been happening in all the realms recently," he said, shaking his head. "Leaderships have been changing hands. Have you read about ghouls?" he asked, changing the subject.

"They're not real," I laughed. He picked up a book from in front of me and turned to a page on ghouls. I couldn't believe it as I began to read.

Ghouls are demon-possessed humans created by demon wolves to rid realms of humans who enter them unlawfully. They can often be manipulated by their leaders to do whatever is asked of them. Once turned, they can drink oleander petals steeped for ten minutes in boiling water to transform back into their human forms. It is a most painful process and can take 48-72 hours to complete. Do not repeat process as death will be inevitable.

"How would humans even find a realm to enter?" I asked.

"Other beings bring them into the realms and hide them. At one time, humans could be granted permission to enter, but under the new demon ruler they are all banned. The new ruler believes humans cannot be trusted to hold the secrets of the realms from the real world."

"Wouldn't realm keepers intervene and stop the demons?"

"Realm keepers only intervene when absolutely necessary," he replied. "Tortuis are the defenses for the realm keepers. They are small emotionless creatures that may appear sweet at first but are truly brutal monsters. Most have never seen them, and those that have disappeared. Tortuis are given orders and permitted to go where and when the realm keepers send them. Everyone is afraid of the tortuis because they work in packs and are next to impossible to stop. They are small, but they have the ability to become invisible, control others, and teleport within twenty feet, among many other abilities the realm keepers provide them," Zane said before leaning in close, making me nervous. "Happy Birthday," he whispered.

I stuttered for a moment as I tried to figure out how he knew. "Thanks," I managed. He stood up and walked towards the door. Before reaching it, he turned back towards me.

"Oh, uh, you might want to look into other monsters while you're at it," he said, chuckling.

"Uh, ok," I mumbled back, still stuttering with a smile on my face. "Oh, hey! Quick question: what's Jane's ability?" I asked.

"No one knows. She won't say. Rosswick thinks she hasn't developed yet," He responded before walking away.

It was really late. I wanted to keep going, but I knew Roger was going to come in soon to shut the lights off. I grabbed a few books and headed back to my room. I wandered down the dark hall and eventually entered my room. I tossed the books on my bed and changed into my night shirt and shorts. The top book was called Monsters of the Realms. I began to flip through it and came across a monster called a golden witch.

Golden witches are demons that appear like angels with black feathered wings with golden tips. They are considered peaceful unless betrayed.

I turned the page to gorgons.

Large ogre-like creatures from the realm Ognaut. They tend to be captured and enslaved for their excellent hunting abilities. What they lack in intelligence and eyesight they make up for with their sense of smell and hearing. They can sniff out the blood pumping through the veins of any living thing and tear them to pieces.

I was surprised to see a beautiful fox on the next page called a myotonic vulpe.

Beautiful monsters that shift from human form to fox when angry or agitated. They are sly, cunning, and mysterious creatures that can escape nearly any trap designed for them.

The passage ended with a warning:

Beware of these creatures when encountered at all costs.

It seemed nearly everything could kill you in these realms.

I figured I'd read about one more before I turned my lights off. That's when I discovered strikers.

Strikers are flying creatures with the ability to explode on impact. They are summoned by rogue demons to conquer realms and instill fear among its people. They are large naked creatures that move like felines but are the size of smart cars.

The warning at the end of the page read:

When you hear the ticking sound, pray as your time is nearly up.

I knew this would be a good place to call it a night. Hopefully in the morning Zane could explain more about these beasts.

The next morning, I found myself training early with Seth. Near the end of our lesson, he paused and looked at me.

"Great job today. I think you're ready," he said.

"Ready for what?" I asked.

"We have another family meeting tonight," he said. "We will go over the mission before you all go out."

I was so excited and nervous I wasn't sure what to say. "Ok, if you think I'm ready," I said hesitantly. He put his hand on my shoulder as he walked me out of the courtyard

"You'll do great, Anya. Don't worry, it's an easy one," he said calmly.

All day I could barely wait. I tried to find Zane, but I couldn't. I ran into Rosswick in the living area.

"Have you seen Zane?" I asked. He lowered his book and looked up at me.

"No, haven't seen him all day. Why are you looking for him?"

"I just wanted to go over some monsters I read about and talk about tonight's meeting with him," I replied.

"Well, when I see him, I will send him your way," he said before picking his book back up to read.

I wandered around the property trying the pass the time. After hours of hiking, I decided to get Jane. I was sure she would have something fun we could do to pass the time. I looked for her in all her usual places, but she was gone too. I realized I was on my own for the day and headed back to the library to return the books I had taken.

Later that night, Zane and Jane seemed to have found their way back as I saw them in the conservatory waiting for the meeting to begin. Finally, Seth arrived, and the meeting began.

"You should all be ready to go first thing in the morning for your mission," he announced.

"Is Anya ready for a mission like this, with all that's going on in the realms?" Rosswick shouted out.

"She has had more than enough training and is capable of such a simple task," Seth replied confidently.

Rosswick sat quietly after that, but I didn't feel as if I was ready. I wondered what Rosswick meant by "with all that's going on in the realms." I felt like I wasn't being told everything.

I felt more nervous than ever as I sat there looking at Seth. I began to question my control over my abilities. Jane saw that I was visibly shaken about the mission and came over to comfort me. After the meeting ended, she told me about her first mission out.

"I had only been with the family a few weeks before I went out on my first mission," she said. "Everyone has each other's back out there. We would do anything to help one another."

Jane's story gave me some comfort, and I began to feel more confident. Zane came over to me as Jane finished.

"You have been making great progress. I'm sure you will do great," he said as he put his arm around my shoulder. I could feel my cheeks begin to color as he walked me over to the others, where we gathered to talk and joke.

After we goofed off for a bit, Seth came over to us. "Go to bed. You have an early morning ahead of you. You're leaving first thing," he said with excitement in his voice. We finished up our conversations and said our goodnights before heading off to bed.

I found myself lying in bed staring up at the ceiling, too nervous to fall asleep. Something was up, and I didn't feel comfortable about going on this mission. Hours had gone by, and I knew we would have to be up in a couple more. I closed my eyes and tried to clear my mind. Thoughts about my mom and the good times we had raced through my mind, and before I knew it, I was asleep.

8
REALM OF REFUGE?

The next morning, I woke up to the annoying alarm clock in my room going off. It was so early I could barely open my eyes. I was so tired from the lack of sleep, I staggered as I walked. I managed to get dressed without injury and grabbed my new backpack to load with snacks. I wobbled my way outside to see an old blue Suburban parked out front for us. The sun was beginning to rise, and I could see Rosswick loading his gear in the back. We all piled in and prepared to leave. I sat next to Jane, and Eddy sat on the other side of her.

We were barely in the truck two minutes before Jane started chatting.

"Did you bring the snacks?"

I stared at her with my half-asleep eyes and straight face.

"Yes, I have the stupid snacks," I replied with annoyance.

"Well, someone isn't a morning person" she replied briefly.

She had told me the most important thing about these missions was to always pack enough snacks. She had practically drilled it into my head these past several months. Of course, I brought the snacks. We hadn't even left yet, and it already felt like it was going to be a long ride.

"I always had snacks when we went on our adventures around here," I said to Jane after a few minutes.

"I know, I just wanted to make sure. I may have forgotten to grab some for myself," she said hesitantly.

"How could you forget? You always say that's the most important thing to bring," I shouted back at her.

"I know, I know, but I'm not going back inside now," she laughed.

Packing the snacks for this trip reminded me of the old days back in Australia when I would go out exploring and find new animals to record. I always packed plenty of snacks wherever I went.

This trip, however, was going to be much different. I noticed Seth wasn't coming, but Rosswick said that he never went out on missions. I found it strange that he would send the people he was protecting out on missions by themselves. Rosswick got into the passenger seat when Zane got in the driver side, and we finally pulled out of the driveway and were now on track to our mission.

I fell asleep at some point shortly after we left. I woke up about an hour later to bickering. I felt much more awake as I stretched and noticed the sun was up now. I looked around, and all I could see were fields.

"Is that lipstick on your neck?" Eddy shouted at Rosswick. Rosswick quickly flipped open the mirror hanging above him and begun to rub his neck intensely.

"NO, it's food or something!" he eagerly replied. Zane kept looking towards Rosswick and laughing hysterically as he tried to continue driving straight down the road.

"Guess you weren't just talking to those girls last night," Zane managed to say while laughing. Rosswick was now visibly red with embarrassment.

"Girls last night? Did you guys go to The Clubhouse without me?" Jane said, angry.

"We had a guy's night out to chill before the mission," Eddy quickly replied, trying to calm Jane down. "It was no big deal."

Jane crossed her arms and sat back, angry at the guys. Eddy kept trying to talk with her, but she was ignoring him. He even attempted to flirt with her a bit, and she just looked away. I turned to stare out my window, trying to ignore the fighting and tension in the truck. I lost track of time, watching the countryside go by, and everyone eventually fell silent.

"Where are we going, exactly?" I eventually asked Zane, hours later.

"We're headed for a small town called Hardgate," he replied.

"Where is this place?" I asked.

"It's not something you would find on an ordinary map," Rosswick said.

"Why's that?"

"With the right kind of map, anyone can travel from one realm to another," Zane explained.

"It allows us to find the town and travel to it. Without this map, we wouldn't be able to enter the realm. Different maps are used to enter different realms. The map is like a key to get in the door," Rosswick added.

I remembered reading about realms and how they had portals or gateways. I was excited to actually go through one.

"We are getting close," Zane said. "We should be there any minute now." I looked ahead and couldn't see anything that looked like a town. Open fields and farmland full of cattle was all I could see around us.

"Keep looking ahead," Zane said eagerly. "You should see it soon."

We drove further and further, and I began to see something shimmering up ahead. Once we made it to the shimmer, it was like a wave through the air. My eyes felt like they were shaking, and everything began to blur. Suddenly my body became tingly, like worms were under my skin, and I noticed we were in a different place entirely. Panic took over me as I tried to breathe again. I felt as if I had held my breath for minutes before we had arrived.

"What was that?" I shouted. "It was like being tickled all over!"

"You'll get used to it the more times you do it," Eddy said, giggling. I gazed back with amazement.

We were now on a mountain road heading down towards what looked like a small town. Moments after arriving, there was a large flash of light behind us and the sky in the realm darkened. Zane abruptly pulled over mere feet from the gateway we had just entered.

"What was that?" he asked, looking at Rosswick.

"Let's check it out."

Zane and Rosswick got out and looked back towards the gateway. Jane, Eddy, and I sat in the truck waiting, watching, and wondering what they were doing. They walked back to where the shimmer was as it disappeared. When the guys got back into the truck, they seemed confused.

"We might be stuck here for a while. The portal closed somehow," Zane said.

"I bet you love this," Eddy said to Rosswick

Rosswick didn't seem too concerned about being stuck since he was familiar with the realm. Zane had told me that it was a realm for refugees, where creatures from across all the different realms could seek asylum.

Zane began to drive down the two-lane road that led into the heart of the town. We passed by a post office on our left and a horse training facility to our right. After driving past a Harley Davidson shop, also on the right side, we reached a chain of stores near the center of the town. Looking around, I noticed that everything seemed abandoned.

"Where are all the people?" Jane asked. No one was around, and most of the shops looked closed. Zane pulled up next to a bar.

"I have no clue. I'll run in here and see if anyone is inside," he said as he opened his door. We all opened our doors to go in as well.

"Wait here. I'll be right back," he said.

"We need to get out anyways. My legs are falling asleep," Jane said as she tried to push me out my door.

As we tumbled out, the darkened sky turned to a glowing orange like a horizon. Strange light grey clouds began to roll in, and it started getting dark. It was now very different from when we started this journey earlier this morning. When we left the mansion, the sun was coming up, blinding us, and the skies were clear blue before we entered the shimmer. It had only been a few minutes since we entered the realm, and already so much had changed. As we stood outside, a frigid breeze blew past, giving the town an eerie feeling. We all quickly went inside the bar.

It was very dimly lit and reeked of cigarette smoke. As I choked on my breath, I noticed there was a woman standing behind the bar. She appeared nervous or anxious as we approached her.

"You must be new here?" she asked.

"Yes," Jane quickly replied.

"Well, you picked a hell of a time to come here," the woman replied.

"Why's that?" Rosswick asked, concerned.

"Weird things are happening," she said as she wiped down the bar.

"Why is the town so quiet?" I asked.

"There was an incident a few weeks back. A bus full of people just drove into the woods and vanished. No one has been found. They're dead though, mark my words."

"Why isn't anyone looking for them?" I asked in disbelief "If it was me, I wouldn't be able to stop searching for my loved ones."

"Right after the bus went missing, there was another incident at the police station. An enormous man the size of a cyclops charged into the building with a chain saw and sliced up all the officers," the women said confidently. "That's how I know the people on the bus are dead. I know that man had to have killed those poor people on the bus too."

"What are you doing here if all this is going on?" Eddy asked.

"Life has to go on, and I still need to work and pay my bills, I heard it's rough in all the realms, so where am I supposed to go?"

I thought that everything she said sounded ridiculous—it all seemed so farfetched.

"How could they be missing if you know they were sliced up?" I asked her abruptly cutting Eddy off.

"A young boy escaped from the bus and watched from the woods," she explained.

"Where are all the bodies?" I asked.

"Your guess is as good as mine, honey. They're just gone." She sounded annoyed with all the questions. "Most of the town still believes they're alive and are holding onto that hope."

I looked at Zane, and he knew exactly what I was thinking. We had to check it out. Our mission was to get some stolen things back for Eddy, but we had stumbled into something much more.

A man came out from the back and paused in his tracks.

"New to town?" he asked. The woman nodded, answering for us. "Nice to see some new faces around here. I'm Charley," he responded.

"I'm Zane. This is Anya, Jane, Eddy, and Rosswick." Zane introduced us. "We just stopped in, trying to figure out what was happening here, but we need to get going."

"If there is anything you need, please just let me know," Charley said as he waved us off.

After getting back in the truck, Rosswick drove us over to the police station and parked in a small store parking lot next to it. Eddy pulled some binoculars from under his seat and noticed that there was an officer sitting in a patrol car outside the station. His car was lit up inside from the glow of his laptop. It would be too noticeable to sneak into the station to take a peek with him right there. We decided that we needed a distraction.

"I have an idea," Eddy quickly said. "Drive me back to that gas station that we just passed."

"What are you going to do?" Jane asked. He wouldn't tell us but had us drive him back to the gas station. He insisted Rosswick needed to go with him and told us to go back to the police station and wait for the officer to leave.

They both got out as we pretended to go back to the police station. Zane stopped the truck a little past the gas station as we all watched what Eddy was about to do. Eddy and Rosswick appeared to talk for a minute or two before walking to the side of the building. Shortly after they went behind it, we saw Eddy in a metallic blue speedo running around the building and into the gas station. We all began to laugh, wondering what the heck he is doing.

Once he got inside, we could see him knocking over display racks and jumping up onto the counters, causing havoc. We watched, intrigued, as we noticed Rosswick hadn't come back yet from around the building.

"What in the world are those two thinking?" Zane asked, laughing hysterically.

Rosswick soon returned from behind the building, and as he did, Eddy came bolting out through the front door of the store like a crazy person. We could hear him screaming, but we had no idea what he was saying. The two men from inside the gas station came out holding their door open and waving their hands, shouting at Eddy. Rosswick seemed to play the role of innocent bystander as Eddy began rolling around on the pavement. Rosswick stood near the other two men as he watched Eddy throw his tantrum.

One of the men went back inside after Rosswick yelled something at him. Moments later we could hear the alarm being triggered inside the store. We had to go. Zane quickly pulled out before the guys noticed we hadn't gone back to the police station.

Still laughing, we made it back to the police station as the officer peeled out of the parking lot. Lights and sirens on, he took off towards town. We parked in front of the building and tried to go in the front door, only to discover it was locked. It was now completely dark outside. Somehow, we went from the sun rising when we left the mansion to pitch dark in just a few hours.

I peeked through the windows to see inside. The place looked like a disaster. There were papers scattered everywhere, blood spattered all over the walls and floor, and debris thrown throughout the room. I could see the alarm system that should have been mounted on the wall torn out and hanging, frayed wires sparking.

Zane kicked the front door open, falling into it.

"The door wasn't on its hinges like it should've been," he said, embarrassed and brushing himself off. "The door frame is broken. Someone just wedged it back in place." He pointed out a board on the inside that had been holding the door in place.

Jane and I walked in and saw blood everywhere. The place reeked of something rotting. There was a small room off to the left side that looked like a conference room where the officers may have gathered for meetings. It now looked like it was used as a murder room. It was wrecked, with holes blown through the walls and blood spattered across the white paint.

Walking through the station, we saw numbered cones all over the place—the kind that police use to mark evidence to photograph. Thankfully, the bodies were no longer present, but I could see where they must have laid at some point. Pools of blood stained the carpet. Walking through another room, I found boxes of files marked "Evidence." Jane came in and started looking through some of the boxes.

"What are you doing?" I asked.

"I'm looking for anything good. Doubt anyone would even know it's missing in this mess," Jane said as she moved a couple boxes.

It didn't appear she found anything, and after a few minutes of rummaging, she sat on the floor, pulled out a cigarette, and started smoking. I couldn't help but stare at her in disgust.

"What?" she said. "I need a smoke. This place smells awful."

I started to gag from the smoke. While we argued about the smell, Rosswick and Eddy walked in laughing about something.

"You guys missed the show," Rosswick stated, interrupting us.

"What did we miss?" Jane asked, pretending we hadn't seen it.

"This loon stripped down to his skimpies and freaked out the town," he said, laughing hysterically.

"I wasn't expecting the police to get there so quickly! I had to run through town to get to the south side where I ran through the woods," Eddy managed to say, still laughing.

"We're not going to have much time if you're here and they're looking for you!" I shouted at Eddy.

"Calm down they're going to be searching the woods for a bit," he said before wandering off.

"Craziest thing I've seen in a while," Rosswick said as we watched Eddy walk away.

I hadn't heard from Zane in a while, so I left to go find him. Rounding the corner near the meeting room, I saw him with his eyes closed.

"What are you doing?" I asked quietly.

"I'm going to cast a spell to see what really happened here," he said. "And see who or what could have caused this much damage."

He started the spell, mumbling words I couldn't make out. He stayed frozen in a trance-like state, blankly staring towards a wall, but I could tell he could see much more than just the room.

"I'm getting a bad vibe about this," Eddy whispered, having followed me. "I'll look around, try to be quiet."

As he walked away, I began to search around the room for more clues to what happened. Suddenly, Eddy looked over at me and waved his arms for me to be quiet. I looked at him like he had three heads.

"I'm being quiet," I tried to whisper, but he shushed me before I could finish. He started to quietly go in and out of rooms, looking around each corner cautiously.

9

RUN

When Zane snapped out of his vision, he looked shaken as he described what he had seen. He had seen a younger man who appeared to work at the police station. He was walking around in business attire, moving some boxes labeled "Case Files." An officer in uniform walked in with a box and placed it on the front desk. He was showing everyone the box's contents and laughing about it. The box was full of stuff he had confiscated from a car that he had pulled over earlier. There was a book sticking out which had strange writings on the cover. It looked like an old journal of some sort.

Zane's vision started to get distorted as he noticed a man standing next to him. His vision became foggier, and the man's silhouette became clearer. The man hadn't noticed Zane, which meant he must have cast the same spell as Zane at a point earlier in time.

Zane was seeing a parallel, a split in time where he could see others who had viewed what he was viewing. Zane explained that when the same spell is cast by different people to view the same point in time, the picture becomes hazy, but the people who had viewed it already become clearer. The man then disappeared, as if he was never there. Whatever he was looking for, he must have seen it already.

Zane continued watching as an officer in the vision walked towards the front door like he was leaving. As he went to open the door, it busted off the hinges, knocking him down. A gorgon entered the station. It was huge, with extraordinary muscles. It stood twice as tall as a normal man, with broken chains hanging from its wrists, and its pants were mostly torn and brown with mud. The gorgon stepped on the door, crushing the officer.

People inside began to panic and scatter. The creature looked around for a moment before charging towards them. Some of the officers started to shoot at it. Their bullets bounced off, only angering it further. Another officer ran up to the gorgon to attack it with a baton, but the beast held him up with one hand and ripped his head off with the other. After dropping the officer's lifeless body, it looked at the others.

Everyone was screaming and running to hide. Three officers locked themselves in an interrogation room.

"Don't make a sound," one officer whispered to the others, hiding behind the only table in the room. The second one began to cry. The monster punched its fist through the one-sided glass mirror. Grabbing an officer, it pulled him back through the wall as the man let out a loud shriek. The gorgon bent the officer in half over its enormous head. Zane could hear the gargling sounds coming from him as the creature threw him like a rag doll. Turning its attention to the other two men, the gorgon broke down the door. Taking the officer who was trying to silence the crying man, he furiously threw him into the crying man, killing them both.

As Zane described the end of his vision, I clutched my stomach, trying not to throw up. Eddy returned from clearing the rooms and reminded us that we couldn't stay much longer. He was now worried the remaining officers who were looking for him would eventually come back to the station when they couldn't find him. We quickly decided to go before they came back.

Zane grabbed the box labeled "Evidence" that he had seen in his vision on our way out. He put the box in the back seat of the Suburban and went back to talk to the guys. They decided to spread out and search the perimeter for the creature or any other clues as to where it went. Zane wanted Jane and I to wait in the car in the parking lot next door for them.

"Leave the headlights on, and if the police return, shut them off so we know to be cautious," Zane said before leaving with the others.

After what felt like an hour, I couldn't wait anymore. I was becoming very impatient and started to go through the box Zane put in the back seat. I found the book he mentioned he had seen in his vision. It was a well-bound, old book, forest green, and had felt material with a gold buckle that locked it. I put it in my backpack to look at later and continued rummaging through the box. Nothing else seemed interesting in it, so I laid across the bench seat behind Jane to relax.

Overwhelmed with anxiety waiting for the guys to get back, I decided to pull the book out again to read through it. As I did, Jane started blasting her stupid music through her headphones and tapping to the beat on the steering wheel. The sounds from her heavy music and tapping drove me crazy as I tried to get the buckle on the book to unlatch.

"Jane, the guys should be back by now," I shouted, tapping on her shoulder. She ignored me and continued beating to her music. I started to get that eerie feeling again, so I put the book back in my backpack. As I set it on the floor, I began to hear weird grunts coming from outside the truck.

I then heard a faint scratching sound along the other side of the vehicle. "Did you hear that?" I asked tapping Jane again.

She rolled her eyes at me and continued to jam out to her music. I looked out the window once more, but I couldn't see anything. It was still dark outside, and a fog had rolled in. The scratching sound got louder and louder before it stopped.

"Jane! Seriously, I hear something outside," I pleaded for her to listen. I leaned over into the front seat ripping out one side of her headphones.

"LISTEN!" I yelled. She looked at me in anger.

"So, what am I listening for?" she demanded to know.

Out of the darkness, a man's bloody head began smashing against the window in the back seat. Again and again the head smashed into the window. I started to scream and jumped over the console into the front seat, yelling for Jane to drive off. Jane, who now could see I wasn't lying, had begun to panic. Ghouls were climbing onto the truck now. One of them pushed through the back window, reaching for us. Jane struggled with the keys but couldn't get the truck to start. She kept turning the key and nothing would happen.

"HURRY, HURRY, THEY'RE COMING!" I shouted, smashing my hand on the dash, but the battery had died! Jane looked at me in panic.

"We're going to have to make a run for it," she said. "Run as far as you can, and I'll try to catch up." She got out of the truck, calling to the ghouls to distract them. I saw an opportunity and opened my door, grabbed my bag, and bolted towards the hills and through the woods as fast as I could go.

The ghouls chased after me as I ran through the dark woods. I was fumbling and tripping and could barely see where I was going. In the distance, I saw a house with the front porch light on. As I cautiously neared the home, an overwhelming sensation of relief took over as I finally felt safe. It was silent outside. Not even the bugs were making a sound. The sky had cleared, but it was still dark. I looked up and could see the moon again. For the first time since jumping out of the car, I looked back and saw no sign of anything chasing me.

The front door was slightly ajar, which brought back my fear as I approached. I curiously crept towards it.

"Is anyone home?" I yelled, while trying to peek through the window panel next to the door. Looking around, I pushed the door open the rest of the way and walked in. There was no response to my question. My heart was racing as I looked around the dark home. I was scared, tired, and had so many questions running through my head. Why was this realm so terrifying? Why did the daytime pass by so quickly, in only a few hours? Thinking about Jane, I wondered if she made it out ok as I crept farther in the home. The guys too—I had almost forgotten about them. They never came back to the truck. What if they ran into that gorgon, the ghouls, or something even worse? I feared for Zane and the others.

I walked across the creaky wooden floorboards and into the living room area. I saw the back of what looked like an old lady's head sticking out from above an old recliner. She was rocking back and forth in an eerie way. Her curly, greyish-white hair flowed over the back of the chair. A gun lay across her lap. I saw the butt of the gun sticking out from one side and the barrel from the other. I slowly walked up and tapped her on the shoulder. She turned quickly and looked up at me, hissing in my face. Her body was torn up and pieces of flesh were missing. Half of her lower jaw was completely gone, exposing her rotten decaying teeth. Frightened, I screamed and ran out the door as fast as I could.

As I ran out of the house, I tripped over the door jamb and rolled down the front steps. I jumped up to see a mob of ghouls coming down the hill from the west side of the house. *They must have heard me scream,* I thought. There were hundreds of them charging towards me now. I took off running down the dirt road and turned onto a narrow dirt trail to try and lose them. When I came to a dead end, I had no choice but to just keep running through the thick of the woods. I didn't know where I was or where I was going, but I had to keep running.

10
STAY STILL

I began to hear things that had to be the ghouls rustling around in the woods behind me. It sounded like a lot of things trampling towards me. It was only a matter of time before the ghouls would catch up to me and I would be too tired to run anymore. I ran further and further through the woods. It felt like I had been running for miles. I needed to find somewhere to hide instead. I was afraid I would go too far if I kept running, and no one would be able to find me.

Thankfully the sky was now clear, and the moon was full so I could see quite a ways into the thick foliage. I looked around and saw small bushes and broken branches all around. None were enough to conceal me. Then as I continued, I saw a fallen tree that was caught on some other trees. It provided just enough coverage to allow me to crouch down behind it without being seen. It looked like it had fallen a long time ago. Partially grown into the side of another tree, it was covered in moss and small ferns.

I sat down on the wet dirt and could hear the ghouls getting closer. I couldn't believe they were still following me. They were relentless.

What did they want? What were they going to do to me? I cried silently as I sat there in the dark. I felt like I lost all hope of surviving. I knew that it was only a matter of time before they would find me. I knew I wasn't ready to go on this mission.

The noises from the marching mob of ghouls finally faded, so I carefully stood up and was creeping over the log to check when I saw a ghoul walking right towards me. He stopped before getting to the fallen log and began to look around. I knew he must be their leader because everyone he passed moved out of his way or knelt down for him to pass. He looked like a normal person, not like a ghoul. He walked over to a large rock nearby overlooking everyone. On top of the rock, he stood with no shirt as his muscles gleamed and his leather pants glistened in the moonlight. He wore a wolf mask on his head like a trophy, with a long pelt that dragged down his back. He slammed his staff into the ground as a young girl walked up behind him. Her armor shimmered in the moonlight, and she clanked as she walked.

The girl came to a stop next to him, dressed in all black, with a wolf face helmet on top of her head. She looked like she was ten or eleven years old. The man looked around for a few more seconds before sniffing the air as if something was there. The ghouls stood motionless, waiting and listening to their leader. He looked at the young girl.

"I can smell the witches in town," he said. He looked down over the crowd. "Find anyone with powers or those protecting them and bring them to me," he shouted. "Look everywhere for my book!" The crowd turned and marched back towards town. The girl still standing on the rock said something softly to him before she pulled her wolf mask down, covering her face as she transformed into an actual wolf. *She must be a shifter,* I thought to myself, as she took off into the woods on all fours. The man stood still on the rock, looking around the woods before he eventually walked off quietly into the darkness.

I noticed some of the ghouls looked like the missing person flyers that hung around town. I remembered reading about how ghouls were made, and I was sure Zane would know where to find oleander leaves to help these people. They must have been created to look for humans, but I wondered why they were sent to look for sorcerers. The man with the wolf mask must be a demon shifter, and the girl too. I wondered what his book was. As I thought about it, I realized this must be who Aku warned me about. I bet they somehow got ahold of an enchanted map and made it to this place to hunt sorcerers.

There was no way I was going to follow them back towards town. I waited a bit longer to make sure no one was coming back. I was truly alone for the first time in a long time. No one knew where I was. An overwhelming feeling of abandonment and sadness began to consume me. I knew I needed to find my way back out. I walked through the woods, looking for a road or pathway. I just wanted to get back to the others.

Coming out of the forest, I found myself in an area of town where even more ghouls were wandering around. It was still very dark, but the sky had that orange glow in it again. That eerie feeling was back, and I looked around, finally noticing a ghoul looking right at me. I hid at the edge of the woods just before the road. The ghoul didn't do anything after it saw me but kept walking around. It was strange because earlier they had been out to get me.

I decided to step out of the shadows to see what they would do. I was terrified when I stepped out, but I stood there while a few of them stared back at me and kept going. They kept to themselves and didn't seem to be interested in me anymore. I walked slowly by, trying not to make eye contact. It was like they didn't even notice I existed. There were bushes, cars, and houses on fire all over as I walked further through the town. They were burning down the town looking for something. I could hear the groans of ghouls coming from some of the homes as I passed. I kept walking until I came across a house near the end of the block that wasn't on fire.

I paused and looked around, not sure if I really wanted to go inside. It was dark out, and there were demons and other creatures around. I knew I needed somewhere safe to hide and I had to go in. I pushed myself to walk slowly up the sidewalk and to the stoop. I looked around once more before taking a few steps up. As I approached the door, I heard some noises. I thought I saw a swift red tail run across the kitchen as I peered through the window. After pushing the door open, I surprisingly saw Jane. She was rummaging around in the kitchen, going through cabinets. I ran to her.

"What are you doing here?" I cried. She startled.

"I'm hungry," she replied. "I needed a place to find food before I could continue to look for you."

"Are you alone? I swear I saw something!"

"Yes, who else would be with me" she asked, puzzled at my question. I sat down and watched as Jane raided the kitchen.

"This place sucks," she said.

"I thought I saw a red-tailed creature in here. I almost thought you were a monster," I said laughing.

"Red tail? That's odd, I haven't seen anyone else in here," she replied calmly.

I continued to watch as she began throwing cans off the shelves, looking for something she liked to eat. I couldn't believe she was hungry at a time like this. I pulled out some snacks from my bag and put them on the table.

"Snacks?" I asked with a smirk on my face. She turned and her face lit up. She ran over and began to raid my snacks.

I frantically told her about the ghouls in the woods, but she treated it like an ordinary experience.

"We need to hurry and get back to the police station and find the guys," I said after she had begun to eat. "How did you escape the ghouls anyhow?"

She just laughed obnoxiously.

"What's so funny?" I asked.

"They were only interested in me until you got out of the truck," she explained. "Once you ran off, they left me and began to chase you."

I got angry that she didn't come to help me right away. "You just left me? We're supposed to have each other's backs!" I shouted in anger as I flung the rest of her snacks off the table. We had been like sisters this past year, and for her to think it was funny to leave me for dead really annoyed me. I couldn't contain myself.

"Some friend you are! I can't even look at you!" I got up and sat outside on the top step of the porch. I could hear her shouting something from inside, but I couldn't make out what she shouted. Eventually she stormed out onto the porch.

"I'm sorry, Anya," she said apologetically. "We are friends, and it was wrong of me not to come right away. Forgive me?"

"I guess," I muttered, still frustrated.

"Wait here," she said. She ran down the street trying to open car doors and checking inside them. Jane must have found one she liked because I saw her climb through the window headfirst. She started it up and drove around to me.

"We need to go back into the main part of town and warn the people of the danger coming," I said. "The demons sent the ghouls to find all sorcerers."

"Get in, let's go!" she shouted at me as I ran around to get in.

She drove towards town. "Is that why ghouls are burning houses down?" she asked.

"I'm not sure, but they're probably checking places and burning them down to flush more people out."

When she pulled up to the bar, I jumped out and ran inside. Charley—the bar owner we met earlier—was holding a gun aimed at my face. He was covered in blood and seemed to be panicking. I noticed a young lady with wings standing behind him. She was tall and very pretty with dark hair and dark colored wings. She wore a black leather jumpsuit that seemed to cover all of her but her wings. Once Charley recognized who I was, he put down his gun and explained who the lady was and that she wasn't dangerous.

"Her name is Veronica," he explained. "I'm hiding her from the realm keepers." She followed him as he checked the windows around the bar.

"The ghouls are coming!" I cried.

"This is going to be the end of us all," he said, looking at me with anguish. "There's nowhere left to go." He ran over to the bar and started to stuff rags in bottles he had set up on the bar with some kind of liquor in them.

"What is going on here?" I pleaded for him to tell me.

"Strange things have been slowly happening here in Hardgate. Ever since the demon wolves' leader from Valdekka changed, things have only been getting worse in all the realms," he explained. "Our gate keeper was killed by the new leader because they believed he hid the old demon wolves' leader in this realm."

"This realm is deteriorating over a single person?" I asked, confused.

"No, this is new. The days going by fast and the nights lasting so long, the strange creatures appearing, and ripples from realm world to human world only started when you guys arrived," Charley said.

"When we arrived, there was a flash and the gate wouldn't open. The shimmer was gone," I quickly replied defensively. "We didn't do anything."

I started to hear the sound of a girl's voice behind me, whining. It sounded like she was crying but trying to hold it back. The sound she made sent chills up my spine as I slowly turned around to see the young girl standing just inside the door.

"Do you know where my parents are?" she asked, sobbing. I bent over.

"I don't know. Where did you last see them?" I asked.

"In our neighborhood, as we were running from the monsters." She could barely speak because she was crying so much.

"We can look for them when it's safe to," I replied. "Come with us and we'll help you."

She looked familiar, but I couldn't place where I had seen her. I couldn't leave her with Charley since he seemed to have lost all hope of surviving and was still freaking out.

I had to find Jane. I held the little girl's hand and went outside to see if she was still in the car. She was gone. I went back inside, and of course, she was sitting at the bar drinking away. Jane poured a few shots across the bar for herself and quickly threw them back. She was never one to shy away from a good time. I went up to her.

"We need to go, now!" I pleaded, pulling her off the stool. She leaned back, grabbing the bottle as we left.

"Where are we going to go?" I asked her.

"We could stay at the post office that we passed when we first arrived," she suggested. "It should be safe there, at least for a while."

It was at the far end of town, where no one seemed to be. Jane noticed the little girl as we were about to get into the car.

"What are we doing with her?" she asked.

"We're going to help find her parents when it's safe out," I said.

She rolled her eyes. "Get in, and no more strays," she shouted.

11

TRAPPED

When we arrived at the post office, Jane drove around to the back. I got out of the car first and went to the back door of the building to see if it was locked. I grabbed the handle and tried to open it with no luck. I jiggled the handle a few times in anger before Jane walked up behind me. She swung her sword, breaking out the glass in the door. It was a long narrow panel of glass, enough to stick her hand through and unlock the door.

Inside, it was empty and dark. There was a long hall with a few rooms off from it. Down near the end of the hall, it opened up to where postal workers would help customers. The girl ran in behind us and hid in a corner near the front. She started to cry and curled up in a ball around some sacks of mail. Jane went to look around as I went over and tried to comfort the little girl.

"What's your name?" I asked, but she wouldn't respond. I wondered what she had gone through, especially since she escaped the ghouls. "You're safe now." I whispered as she quieted, falling asleep.

Jane walked around the counter. "She asleep already?"

"Yeah, poor thing must have been exhausted," I replied. "I need to get some rest too."

"I'll take first watch," Jane offered.

I walked across the dark mail room to lay down and rest my head on some of the mail sacks near the front counters. As I lay there, staring up at the tiles, thoughts began racing through my mind, trying to figure out what was happening to Hardgate. We hadn't even been able to think about our original mission. I wondered where the guys were, and if they were safe. I couldn't deal with this anymore. I just didn't know how everyone else could handle this so well. I'd finally made friends, only to fear losing them in a place like this. I'd started to feel like I was part of this weird family, and the thought of dying was overwhelming.

Almost three hours later, I woke up dazed and confused as I saw daylight shinning down on me from the window nearby.

"Wake up!" a strange man shouted at me. I rolled over, looking up at him. "Are you going to get my stamps?" He spoke in a raspy old voice. All I could do was stare at him, confused. Why in the world would he want stamps at a time like this?

I quickly stood up, looking around for Jane and the little girl. I didn't see them anywhere.

"Well? Can you?" the man asked again, but with frustration in his voice. I rushed to get out of the back door before anyone else saw me.

Pushing the back door open, I noticed the glass was now fixed. There was no way someone had already replaced it. I looked it over again to confirm it was the same door that Jane broke last night. Opening the door all the way I was immediately blinded by the bright sunlight beaming me in the face. I pulled my arm up to block the sun and realized it was warm and muggy out like it was in New Zealand. Overwhelmed with emotions of being out of the nightmare and wondering if it was all a dream, I heard something. I looked around, trying to block the bright sun as a man yelled at me.

"HEY! You're not supposed to be back here. This is a restricted area," he cried.

Still confused, I ran off into the brush straight behind the post office. *What is going on?!* I thought to myself. As I ran, I noticed the same shimmer we crossed through when we entered the realm. I ran through it and didn't seem to notice much of a change, but I was focusing on getting away from the man at the post office. When I felt I had gone far enough to be out of sight, I stopped. I realized I was nearly a football field away, and I crouched down in the tall grass. I looked back towards the post office to make sure the man hadn't followed me and noticed a cold breeze suddenly blow by.

Puzzled as to why it felt like I was back in the real world, I felt something slithering around my waist. Before I had a chance to look down, it began to get tighter and tighter. I finally looked down and grabbed ahold of what looked like vines wrapped around me as I struggled to turn around. More and more vines reached out like tentacles trying to grab my legs. I tried to scream, but it was squeezing all of the air out of my lungs. As I gasped for more air, I remembered my katana and tried to get it out. I struggled to free one arm and began slicing at the vines a few times. Rolling around in the dirt I managed to get my legs free before It started to squeeze tighter around my waist. It twisted up and around my arm as I struggled to break free from it once more. I wielded my katana with my free arm and managed to escape. It released me, and I crawled along the dirt to get away.

I stood up and was surprised when I saw the rest of it. A large plant was trying to consume me. I ran back through the brush towards the post office once again. Rushing through the brush, I was in disbelief. Whatever it was, that creature wasn't in any of the books I had read. I wondered why the hell it had seemed for a moment like I was back in New Zealand and everything was normal. I remembered the shimmer I ran through and wondered if I had gotten out of Hardgate and unknowingly ran back in. This place was truly unusual and nothing like I had read in any of the books Zane had me study.

Finally making it back to the post office, I saw Jane walking out of the back door. As I approached her, she was alone and smoking another cigarette with her back up against the building and her foot on the wall. I walked over to her as she looked me up and down and smirked

"What happened to you?" she asked.

"I was almost eaten by a plant," I said angrily. "WHAT JUST HAPPENED?" I yelled at her, as Jane starred at me with confusion. I told her what happened when I woke up and how the door was fixed, and how I was almost eaten by the plant.

"I believe this realm is experiencing tremors from the gateway being broken," she said confidently. "I've heard about them happening and people crossing in and out of the realm, but that's all I know"

"How is that possible?" I screamed.

"I'm not sure." She looked at me in shock. "But we need to get out of here. I've heard about realms disappearing after events like this." Jane seemed very worried about the realm being destroyed while we were still inside it. I feared what would happen to us if that happened.

"Where's the little girl?" I asked after realizing she wasn't around.

"She was gone when I noticed you were gone," Jane said quickly. "I looked around for you both, but I figured she was with you."

My feelings about the strange little girl were tentative. I felt like I had seen her somewhere before but couldn't remember where. I was confused where she may have ended up. If I went back to New Zealand, where did she go?

"We should look for her" I said concerned.

Jane tried to play it off like it was no big deal. "I'm sure she's fine. I'm more concerned that the car is gone. I bet that little girl probably stole it," she said.

"I just want to go home now," I muttered. "I'm so over this mission." I stormed off in the direction of town.

"Are you coming?" I yelled back to Jane.

"Wait up!" she yelled as she tossed her cigarette and jogged to catch up to me.

We headed back to Charley's bar. No one was around. As we walked, I noticed the sun was still shining but not nearly as bright as it was when I left the post office. The sky seemed to have strange, darkened red clouds moving in and cold air blowing through. It was still early in the morning, but at least the sun was up. Things appeared to be normal once we entered the bar, creepily normal. It was like last night never happened. There were a few people inside, drinking as if the world wasn't falling apart. We looked at each other in shock that people were inside so early acting ordinary. We slowly went over to the bar.

As we sat down, Zane saw us from a corner table he had been sitting and came over. He sat next to Jane, who immediately tilted her head and rested it on his shoulder. I rolled my eyes at Jane in jealousy.

"The things we saw last night were insane. You guys would have gone nuts," Zane said in his soft-spoken voice. "I followed Eddy through the woods, tracking the beast from the station when we came across something crazy."

I looked at him, intrigued "What did you guys find?"

He paused for a moment. "I need your help, Anya."

"My help? Why do you need my help?" I replied unwillingly.

He paused, before finally speaking again. "I think if we combine our powers together, we can find the creature. We were tracking it when suddenly it vanished. I tried to cast a vision spell, but it wasn't enough to find it. I think that together we could channel our powers and find it."

"Why do you care so much about finding this creature?"

"We believe it is the beast that stole Eddy's realm relics," he replied.

"We should stay together anyways. I guess I'm in," I quickly responded.

After I agreed to go, Zane told us there was no way out of this realm that he could find. All the exits were blocked off, and we were stuck here unless we could get that portal opened again. He said the portal map wouldn't open the portal, no matter what he and Eddy tried. He went on to say that he had no idea where Rosswick was either.

"We need to find Rosswick," I said. "He's familiar with this realm and probably knows a secret way to get out."

Zane decided we should go back to the police station first to see what else we could find or figure out. Jane insisted she stay at the bar and told us to go on without her. We left and walked through some residential neighborhoods to get there. Zane showed me some amazing things he had found the night before. He pulled out what looked like an old metal key, one that would unlock dungeons centuries ago.

"What is that for?" I asked as he chuckled.

"It's a crypto key. It can unlock doors and other things with locks." I noticed the key had a magical shimmer in his hand. It reminded me of the map we used when we first arrived. It also reminded me of the book from the truck.

"You should have read about these. Powerful mages can use ancient spells to enchant items like this. They're rare to find," he said as he grasped the key tightly and put it in his pocket.

He dug in his other pocket and pulled out some interesting stones that he found when they were tracking the creature. The stones were little pebbles, but some were marbled with white and pink while others were white and blue. I started to tell Zane about the book when he stopped me. He was staring at something up ahead.

"What do you see?" I asked.

"I'm not sure."

We continued slowly through another rural area. Zane saw a house that seemed to interest him, and he wanted to take a look around.

"I have to go in," he insisted.

"I've only had bad experiences going into homes around here," I said with great concern. "The ghouls could be hiding in there."

Zane just shrugged me off though. "I've seen this house before—in a dream I had last night," he said with a surprised look on his face.

"We can just pop in really quick and be out before anything even knows we were inside," he said with excitement.

"Ugh...alright but we need to be quick," I groaned.

We slowly crept up the steps and over to the window. Peeking in, we saw a man wearing black pants with no shirt on hunched over a table fiddling with something. He had a bunch of symbols tattooed all over his back. They appeared to be a chain of arrow heads going down his spine and had chains coming out and around. There were dark sections filled with smaller patterns that were hard to make out. Some looked like Maori words I had studied back home in the library.

The man seemed to be carving something into a block of wood, but we couldn't tell what it was. When I noticed his wolf mask sitting on the table, I began to panic. I thought he looked familiar. At that moment, Zane was about to cast a spell to see what he was doing, but before he could I quickly grabbed him to stop.

"This is the leader of the ghoul people," I whispered. "He'll kill us. He hunts people by sensing their energy. He can sniff the air and find people with magic that way."

"How is that possible?" Zane asked, shocked.

"Let's go," I said, tugging at his arm.

We quickly ran towards the woods for safety. I told him all about what I had seen and heard yesterday in the woods—why the people were going missing around town, and the man and little girl in the woods.

"We could have been killed," I lectured. "We need to be more careful. This is what Aku warned me about back home." Suddenly, I froze.

"What's wrong?" Zane asked.

"You won't believe this," I said, still trying to wrap my brain around it all.

"What?" he asked with excitement "What, Anya?"

"I knew that little girl looked familiar."

"What little girl?" he asked, confused.

I told him about the little girl that came up to me looking for her parents and how Jane and I took her with us to the post office. I told Zane how she looked so much like the little girl from the woods, but she was dressed like a normal child.

"Where is she?" he asked

"She left in the middle of the night," I said confused.

"Well, she's gone now," he said. "Don't worry about it."

We continued our journey back down the road where it seemed safe. I couldn't help but wonder about the little girl and if she really was the girl from the woods or not. Walking towards the police station, Zane walked closely by my side as we talked about the mysteries this place held. I could feel myself getting flustered.

12
NEW THREATS

We had almost made it to the woods at the end of the street when I saw three large shadows dart through the sky over our heads. I tried to see what they were, but they flew past too quickly. Zane looked at me.

"Did you see what it was?" he asked.

"I don't know, they flew by too fast," I said. "Whatever they were, they must not have seen us since they didn't stop." I was fairly certain about that.

"It was probably just strikers," Zane said, like it was supposed to be no big deal.

We continued to walk, but all I could think about was the strikers and what I had read about them back at the mansion. They were ugly flying creatures that divebombed targets, exploding on impact. They could also use their tentacles like arms to shoot tar like substances that could melt skin.

After passing through a small trail in the woods, we were almost to the police station. Thankfully, I could see some stores up ahead even though it was getting dark out again.

"The sun was only up for a few hours," I said. "I wonder how it keeps getting dark so quickly."

"I've never seen anything like it before," Zane said. "I'm not sure what's happening.

I asked Zane where we were going as I noticed we had changed directions. He seemed to have lost interest in finding the creature but now wanted to see the strikers that flew overhead.

"I just want to see them. I've never seen them alive."

The sky was already darkening, even though it was hardly noon.

"We need to find Rosswick while we're out here," I told him. I wondered where he had gone since we last saw him at the police station. Zane agreed, and we traveled through the back streets along the edge of the woods outside one of the neighborhoods.

Walking along the road closest to the woods I kept getting that eerie feeling again. Suddenly, Zane stopped and looked back at me.

"MOVE!" he yelled. A large shadow swung out from the treeline, grabbing me by one leg, knocking me to the ground. It started to drag me into the dark woods. A terrifying emotion overwhelmed me, and I could barely say anything. It happened so quickly it knocked the air out of my lungs. I screamed out for Zane and grasped for anything I could. I couldn't tell what it was, but it had a tight grip on me.

I was grabbing fists full of dirt as I tried to save myself from this monster. Zane finally reached for his katana and swung at the shadow beast, but that didn't seem to faze it at all. *This is not how I wanted to die,* I thought to myself. Not here, not today. I started to think about my mom and how I wanted to see her again. I wanted to be back in Australia with her. I became angry and scared all at the same time. I didn't know what to do, and I began to panic. I was so afraid this was the end.

Desperately grabbing ahold of some roots, I held on tight. With my adrenaline pumping, I pulled myself forward, struggling to my feet. I felt this sudden surge of energy pulsing through my entire body like I'd never felt before. I could see a glow radiating from my skin like I was some kind of radioactive ghoul. I started ripping and clawing at the monster's tight grip around my ankle.

Zane managed to slice off one of its limbs with a single swing of his sword, but it was still wrapped around my leg. I bent down to remove it, but as I did it slowly started to disappear. It was as if it melted into the ground, and before I knew it, it was gone. Zane looked at me in amazement.

"I've never seen anything like that before," he said.

"What do you mean?" I asked, confused.

"You must have harnessed your energy and manifested it somehow. When you started to get angry, you began glowing. We have to tell Seth when we get home," he said excitedly. I brushed myself off and grabbed my backpack off the ground.

We continued heading towards the strikers. With every turn of the path we took, we cautiously made sure it was clear ahead before proceeding. We never saw the shadow creature again, but I was still petrified and shaken by what had happened and terrified that it might come back. I kept thinking about the monster, wondering why it picked me to attack and not Zane.

"I still can't believe what happened back there and how you just pulled yourself up like that." Zane couldn't stop talking about what I had done as we passed street after street. After what felt like miles of walking, we saw an abandoned car that looked drivable. A vehicle would make getting around so much faster and safer, especially since Jane left ours at the police station. We got up to the car, but the doors were locked. Zane remembered the crypto key and pulled it out with excitement. After a few seconds of fidgeting, the door unlocked easily. We got in, and Zane tried to start it, but the engine wouldn't turn over. He kept trying until the key got it started. I was happy that I didn't have to walk the rest of the way.

"Where are you going?" I asked.

"We're going to see where the strikers were going," he said, confused by my ignorance.

I sat there, less excited. I had forgotten we were tracking those things. We traveled through town in the direction we saw the strikers flying. As we neared the post office, Zane figured that this must've been where they were going.

We pulled into the empty parking lot. It was pitch dark outside now, and the only lights were coming from a street nearby. Looking at the car's clock, I saw that it was only one fifteen in the afternoon.

"This is getting weird," I said. "Have you noticed that it's only when it's dark out or it's getting dark that the people disappear and the demon monsters come back?" He was about to say something when we saw an enormous cow-like skull towering over us about ten feet off the ground. No legs or body, just a dimly glowing skull. It didn't make any noise or touch the ground. It was slowly floating through the empty parking lot. I began to panic, and I screamed. The skull turned towards us and stopped, like it was about to charge.

"Don't move," Zane said.

We stared at it for a few moments. After a couple of terrifying minutes, it started to hover towards the other side of the lot. Zane put the car quietly into drive and pulled out of the parking lot slowly. We drove back into town once again. I kept looking back but that thing didn't seem to have noticed or followed us as we left.

"Hold on," Zane said.

Suddenly he veered off the main road and drove through a dirt trail close to where we had come from.

"What are you doing?" I shouted.

"I think I saw something," he said as he continued to drive. He followed the trail, and it took us through another small, wooded trail that led to a paved back road into a nearby neighborhood. He abruptly stopped and got out of the vehicle without saying a word, leaving his door open. I didn't know what was going on. I got out and followed him.

"Where are you going?" I kept asking him, but he just kept walking, focused on something. When he stopped, I jogged up to him.

There was another enormous beast lying there, but this one was crushed to death. The beast was thirty or forty feet long with large tusks, covered in grey fur and built like a gorilla. It looked as if it weighed a couple of tons. It seemed like it should have been impossible to kill, yet somehow it was crushed like a bug. I wondered what could've killed it. I didn't think either of us really wanted to know.

"It's the beast Rosswick and I ran into earlier," Zane told me. "It's a rare species called *peludo bestia*, but it was believed to be extinct."

"I don't remember reading about it," I replied. "What does this mean for Eddy's things?"

"They come from a fairytale realm that most people don't believe exists called The Lost Realm. Only a handful of people say they have actually been to it, and most don't believe them," he said, looking over the body. "I'm sure Eddy won't be getting his things back now."

"How can a creature from a place like that end up in the Hardgate realm?" I asked, confused.

"I don't know," he said. "I saw the footprints on the side of the road. That's why I followed the trail that led us here. When Rosswick and I saw this creature earlier today, we knew we were no match for it. We had to sneak away so it wouldn't see us."

I realized what he was getting at. There was something stronger and larger out here that killed it, something that we definitely were no match for. We rushed back to the car in case it was nearby and drove off quickly.

Driving down the dark road, we saw a little house coming up with a light on outside. It looked like a good place to rest for the evening. We feared there was no way we would make it back to Jane in the dark without running into the creature.

"This one looks like a safe one," Zane said as we drove up to a house. It was a two-story home that didn't appear too damaged or on fire like some of them were. The home was made of brick, with a six-foot metal fence around it.

"Keep a lookout. Make sure nothing is following us before I pull in," Zane said. I looked all around and made sure we were safe.

"Your good" I replied, sitting back down in my seat. No lights were on inside that I could tell, but the porch light was on, and the gate was open. Zane pulled in and parked outside the porch, off to the side of the house.

"Maybe the family left in a hurry?" I asked before we slowly got out.

13

SOMETHING LURKING IN THE DARK

Walking up to the door, I got that strange feeling again that something was wrong. Zane must have too because we both stopped and looked at one another.

"Let's go in silently and make sure it's clear before we make too much noise," he said quietly. I nodded as he slowly opened the front door and cautiously entered. Once inside, we branched off, checking the home to make sure it was empty. Zane went left from the doorway, and I went right. I entered the living and dining area, but the room appeared empty, so I slowly went on to check the rest of the home. I went to meet Zane in the hallway after he cleared his side of the first floor.

While Zane went to check out the front door to make sure nothing was coming outside, I moved back towards the stairs to check the second floor. A noise stopped me in my tracks. I heard a loud sniffing sound like a bear that sent chills shooting down my spine. I waved frantically to get Zane's attention. When he looked over at me, I started to make a shushing motion. I could tell from the way Zane's eyes widened that he could hear the sniffing sound now too. I pointed up, letting him know that it was coming from upstairs. I remained frozen in my tracks, too scared to go check while Zane tried to tiptoe over to me.

"We should leave," he whispered. I nodded but a part of me wanted to see what it was.

Walking towards the front door, we heard something coming down the stairs, and we quickly scrambled to hide. I was desperate to get out of sight as fast as possible and jumped over the back half of the couch. I watched as Zane ran to a closet under the stairs. I threw a blanket over myself. When I heard the closet door open, I peeked my head up and saw Zane quietly motioning for me to get in the closet. I started to rush towards it to hide. As I did, I could see what looked like a dog's shadow slowly coming down the stairs. It was looking around and sniffing for something. Its shadow reminded me of the man in the woods with the wolf mask.

As it appeared, I froze in place near the closet. I could tell that it was a wereman. It had human hands and feet but walked on all fours. As it slowly walked down the stairs, I could see that it was extremely tall. Its body was boney and lengthy, covered in hair down its face and backside. It was hairless down its arms and legs. Its hind legs were bent in a dog like stance, but it was very human-like in appearance. I watched it pick up objects as it stopped on the first landing of the stairs, looking under a flowerpot and books that were on a stand and tossing them aside, it looked like it was searching for something specific. I managed to get in the closest unseen and unheard. Zane closed the door slowly and locked it.

"This is what Rosswick thought he saw in the woods behind the police barracks," he whispered.

I couldn't help but shudder at the thought of what it would do if it found us.

Its steps got closer until it stopped in front of the closet, sniffing the air again. We both were paralyzed with fear and tried to hold our breath as we heard it right outside the door. Finally, we could hear its steps getting farther away as it walked off. I was terrified that it was going to smell us. I started to whisper to Zane when suddenly something slammed against the wall on the back side of the closet. Zane jumped, and I let out a shriek, practically jumping in Zane's arms. A hand punched through the wall just over my head. Zane flung the closet door open and pushed me out as we made a run for it.

We ran out the front door and towards the car. I jumped in the driver's seat while Zane tossed me the key. I tried to start the car as Zane slid across the hood before getting in. The wereman busted through the front door and stood on his hind feet, howling from the porch before coming after us. I started to panic as I fumbled with the key to start the car. The wereman jumped on the hood, pounding its fists at the roof of the car over and over. It struck the windshield, breaking the glass and tearing part of it away. I finally managed to get the car started and slammed it in reverse, spinning backwards in a circle, crashing through the fence and into the neighbor's brick house. The wereman flipped off the hood and onto the roof of the car.

I quickly put the car into drive and peeled out of the yard onto the street. Zane pulled out a shot gun with a short barrel. I tried to stay focused, but I was surprised by the gun that he had in his leather coat. He loaded it quickly and began shooting the wereman.

"Hold on," I shouted at Zane as we approached a corner. I sped up and decided to do a quick turn to toss the wereman off the roof. As we took the turn, the car slid, and we rolled a few times off the road's edge and down into the woods, eventually coming to a stop.

The wereman was flung off into the darkness. Zane was thrown from the car and somehow landed in a tree unharmed. I was still in the car and in a lot of pain. The air bag never deployed, and my head hit the steering wheel, breaking my nose. Blood was pouring everywhere. I was dazed and confused as I tried to open my door, but it was crushed in. My window was shattered, so I willed myself to climb out, falling onto the ground. As I lay there, I saw Zane up in the tree still holding his shot gun and looking around for the wereman.

"Can you see it?" I yelled at him.

"No, I can't," he said.

I started to pull myself up while Zane climbed down from the tree. He rushed over to me, making sure I was alright before heading back to the passenger side of the car. He quickly loaded his gun again.

I was wiping the blood from my face when I heard a cracking sound. I quickly turned toward the noise and saw the wereman running towards me. Zane shot at it, which only seemed to confuse it and piss it off even more. It continued to charge at me. I turned around to run and tripped over a branch, falling to the ground, hitting my knee on a rock. In excruciating pain, I grabbed my knee. The wereman was still charging towards me, and finally I felt my adrenaline kick in. I started to scoot backwards to escape, but I wasn't fast enough. The wereman ran up and snatched me off the ground. I struggled to escape, punching at its arm, but its grip was just too tight. Zane tried to fire once again, but the gun jammed.

The wereman growled in my face as I watched the saliva drip from its mouth. All I could smell was the stench of roadkill mixed with trash on a summer day as it breathed on me. Then I remembered the first spell I learned, *Encanto*—to move or eliminate matter around me. I looked down at the ground, concentrating on the dirt. The wereman was shaking me as it turned to growl at Zane. It turned back to bite at me, but the dirt below started to disappear. I had managed to make a hole that was about fifteen feet deep and ten feet wide. As it caved in, the wereman fell, letting go of me to save itself. I managed to catch the edge of the hole grabbing ahold of some roots near the rim with one hand.

I was losing my grip when Zane ran over and reached for my arm. We could hear the wereman growling from below. I screamed as Zane yanked me up out of the hole. We fell back, and I landed on top of him, holding on tight.

"I thought we were going to die," I cried, lying there.

"We have to get out of here," he said, helping me up.

Zane ran back to the car to see if it would start, but it was no use. The car was totaled. Zane grabbed our gear, and we headed back up to the road. My knee was bleeding and starting to swell, and my face was still bleeding some, but I managed to climb back up to the street with Zane's help. I didn't have a choice—we had to keep moving.

14

WANDERING SUPER WOLVES

Once we were out of the woods and back on the road, we looked to see if anything was following us. If the wereman had made it out of the hole, he must not have seen which way we went. Zane had me hold onto his arm to help me walk. We started to follow the street back past the house we came from and into the heart of town. It took much longer with my swollen knee. We didn't see or hear anything unusual, which made me nervous. So far on this mission, when things seemed fine, they ended up going really badly. We saw Charley's bar up ahead with the lights on. As we got closer, we could see people inside. We looked at each other in relief and hurried inside.

We saw Jane first, still sitting at the bar and acting like her normal self. She was flirting with another patron, while her head was resting on another man's shoulder. When she saw us, she jumped up and rushed over. Visibly intoxicated, she staggered towards us, tripping on a stool leg and nearly falling. I reached out to catch her as she found her way, laughing.

"What happened?" she asked. "You guys look like shit."

She stared at me in shock, noticing all of the blood on my face and shirt. Then she pulled me over to a table, and I sat down while she started to clean my face with a wet dish rag.

"I want to keep watch," Zane said, heading back to the door. "Make sure we weren't followed."

"Who did this?" Jane asked, concerned.

I didn't understand what she meant at first. I wondered why she thought someone would break my nose.

"Who would do this to me?" I asked sarcastically.

"Zane didn't do this, did he?" she asked, puzzled now. I wondered to myself what she was talking about.

"No, nothing like that happened! We were attacked, and we've been on the run most of the time."

"You and Zane, on the run alone?" she asked, smirking. "The two of you have any fun together?"

"What are you talking about, Jane? We were a bit too busy trying not to die to enjoy ourselves."

"Sure, whatever you say," she said. "I know you're not so innocent, Anya. I know you like Zane."

I really didn't know what she was getting at, but I didn't want to argue with her while she was drunk. I could feel my face turning red.

"Whatever," I said before walking away. I thought Zane was attractive, but still didn't want to tell him that. I thought about it and realized maybe I did want to say something. I walked over to Zane, who was looking out the window near the front door.

"I want to go back to the church where we'll be more protected," he said. "Churches are protected by certain spirits. Maybe we'll find Rosswick there too, since he knew the minister years ago when he was a kid." Zane sounded exhausted.

Jane eventually came over and leaned on Zane. "Oh, I spoke... Who did I speak—ha, ha, I spoke to Seth while you two were gone," Jane managed to say, tripping over her words. We were grabbing our stuff from the floor near the front door when we quickly stopped.

"He uh... said not to worry, uh... and that he'd find a way to get us all out."

I felt an overwhelming sense of relief when I heard that Seth was working on a way to get us out of this hellhole.

"Imma stay here... in case he calls again," Jane said as she laughed.

"I'm not sure that's a good idea Jane," I said, concerned. "You really should come with us."

"No, I'll stay here—be fine," she muttered as Charley walked over.

"I'll keep an eye on her. I know she has been obsessed with the phone, asking every time it rings," Charley said calmly as he wiped out a beer mug with a small towel.

"If it gets crazy, get to the church," Zane said, deeply concerned.

Before leaving, I walked over to Jane, who sat back at the bar. "Please try to sober up some," I said before walking away.

"Yeah, yeah, whatever," she shouted at me.

Zane and I left and headed over to the church. I wanted to tell him how I felt about him, but I was too afraid to. The streets were quiet, and for once we didn't run into trouble. As we neared the church, we could see Rosswick talking with a man in all black at the side of the building. I figured he must be the minister. When we got closer, we could overhear what they were saying.

"Head inside," the minister was saying to Rosswick. "There are blankets and lots of food. Please help yourself." He looked over at us as we crossed the street.

"It's all free if you need it," the minister said. "People donate food to the church. We have more than enough supplies."

He reached out and shook both our hands. "I'm David, the church minister," he said.

"David, nice to meet you," Zane said. "Can we talk?" He pulled David aside.

Rosswick looked over at me in shock.

"I can't believe someone as green as you is still alive after all of this," he said.

I was initially flattered, but as I thought about it, I realized it was an insult.

We started to talk about what had happened to each of us. We contemplated where Eddy could be since no one had seen him recently.

"Hope he found his treasures that were stolen," Rosswick said.

"Probably not," I quickly replied. "Zane and I found the creature that stole them, and he was dead."

"You found the creature! And something killed it?" he replied in shock.

Zane came back over to us, while the minister walked away from the church and down the street.

"You found the creature that took Eddy's things?" Rosswick asked Zane.

"Yes, the same creature I saw in my vision that took his treasures," Zane responded.

"Where is David going?" I asked Zane.

"He had to go do something, but wouldn't say what," Zane said. "Do you hear that noise?"

At that moment, the cellar doors next to us at the side of the church burst open. Rosswick looked at us in fright.

"Did the wind just do that?" he questioned.

"We should close them before David gets back," I suggested. I didn't want him to think we were snooping in his basement.

"It's not windy enough for that," Zane answered Rosswick.

We all walked over to the cellar doors, and as we reached out to close them, they slammed shut. They were heavy steel doors and far too heavy for the wind to blow.

"Someone should go check it out," I suggested.

We argued who should go first, but no one wanted to go. Standing to the side of the cellar, I slowly opened the door. Looking over I could only see down a few wooden steps. It was still too dark to see, even with the moonlight. The cellar steps appeared dirty and rotten. The guys were still arguing over who was going to go down first. I took a couple steps and mocked them for chickening out. Rosswick got brave and went four steps down, a couple past me. The stairs were very narrow, and it was a tight squeeze for Rosswick to get past me. Zane stayed at the top, outside of the cellar, looking down at us.

"Feel around and see if you can find the light switch," I told Rosswick.

As he felt around, I saw a pair of glowing red eyes appear at the bottom of the stairs. I grabbed Rosswick's shoulder in fear.

"Rosswick, look," I said. The eyes didn't appear to be moving.

"It's probably just a breaker light," he laughed.

Then another pair of glowing eyes appeared, and something began to growl, the sound echoing throughout the cellar. It was too dark to tell what it was. I heard Rosswick gasp, just as the eyes started charging towards us up the stairs. Rosswick panicked to get out of the cellar and ran up the stairs past me. As he did, I grabbed his shirt in panic, pulling him backwards to get by him. I made it up the stairs first and jumped out of the cellar as fast as I could.

"It's a super wolf!" Zane yelled, as it snatched Rosswick, who was trying to stand back up. It dragged him into the darkness by his leg. He screamed out in pain, falling to his stomach as he disappeared. Running back down the stairs I reached out to grab ahold of his hand, but it was too late.

Rosswick was gone. I ran back out in fear I was next. Zane just looked at me in shock as we heard Rosswick's screams from the darkness below. Zane pulled two nine-millimeter pistols from his jacket.

"He's still alive," Zane shouted before he ran down the stairs and began firing into the darkness. I could see glimpses of Rosswick's silhouette in the flashes of Zane's shots. Suddenly, Rosswick fell to his side.

"You shot me," he shouted at Zane.

As more shots from the guns rang out, I could see that Rosswick had a hunk of flesh missing from the back of his leg near his butt, and a bullet wound in his shoulder. He was also missing a chunk of skin from his side. He was now covered in blood, and I feared he wasn't going to make it out in time.

15

FIND DAVID

Walking down the cellar stairs, I cast *Ackura*, the light spell, which would illuminate the cellar. My first cast created a spark but didn't light up the room long enough. I repeated the spell and aimed it in the direction of Rosswick's cries. The spell worked and finally lit up the room from right above his head. That was when I realized it wasn't such a great idea. With the room well-lit, we could see everything that was in it. Not only could we see everything, but everything could see us.

Frozen in fear, we all stood there. I will never forget the look on Rosswick's face when he looked around. He looked back at me with this look of distress and fear as if all hope was gone from him. The room was full of super wolves, not just the two we had all thought. They all turned and focused on the three of us. Their heads were low and their backs up high. The fur down their spines stood straight up as they growled and nipped at us. I got back-to-back with Rosswick and Zane.

We counted five super wolves. They were surrounding us, and there was nowhere to escape. I pulled out my katana and started slashing at the wolves to keep them back. My adrenaline was pumping as I managed to slash one across the face. It didn't seem to do much damage. It whimpered and backed up at first, then went right back into attack mode. Zane started shooting his pistols again. He managed to take down two of the wolves. However, this just seemed to anger the other three. Rosswick did all he could to just stand near us.

I cast Encanto, the matter eliminating spell that I had used earlier on the wereman. A large hole opened up, swallowing the other three wolves. I was shocked by how quickly I was able to do it this time. I heard the whimpers of the wolves echoing throughout the cellar. I was so relieved. Finally, I felt like we were safe. Zane started to fire a few shots into the hole at them.

"Zane, leave them! Let's go," I pleaded, trying to hold Rosswick up.

Zane turned and looked at us both. "RUN," he yelled. We all began to run, even Rosswick with his adrenaline pumping once again. Zane made it up the stairs first, and I was right behind him. The light spell died out, and I looked back, but I couldn't see Rosswick anymore. Then we heard a loud thud followed by Rosswick moaning. He had fallen into another hole I must have created accidently. He was far too weak and hurt at this point to make it out on his own.

Zane quickly cast his agility spell, *Zumada*, which I had never heard before. It increased his speed by about six times his normal rate. He looked at me.

"I'm going to get him. Shut the door behind me," he said as he ran down the stairs towards Rosswick. I slammed the door quickly and held it shut. As soon as I did, I felt something smash against the door from the other side. One of the super wolves must have made it out of the hole and ran into the door as I closed it.

I was sitting on the grass outside the cellar doors when I heard something rustling from inside. I stood up in a panic, thinking that a wolf was coming. Instead, Zane busted out from the cellar doors, carrying Rosswick over his shoulder. He looked like a flash of light as he came busting out. My heart stopped for a moment as he slammed the doors shut behind him. I was elated to see he had gotten Rosswick out.

Running with Rosswick was no easy task. Rosswick may have been thin and tall, but he always carried a lot of armor, weapons, and books, so that he was always prepared for anything. With all of that on him, he must have weighed close to 300 pounds. Zane managed to lay him down onto the grass next to the cellar doors. He was unconscious now and not responding. I was afraid he was going to die without any real help.

Zane cast a spell using David's full name to find out where he was at that exact moment. I never had figured out how to do that spell correctly. I could never remember its name to even attempt it. I could only hope that one day I would know as much as Zane did.

"I saw a chalk board with writings on it and a desk," Zane said, staring at me. "He must be at the school. Get in the church and block all the doors. Stay with Rosswick and keep him safe. I need to get David. He'll know how to help Rosswick. If Rosswick comes to and can walk, try to get him to the gas station in town."

Zane put his hands on my shoulder. "You can do this," he said as I stood there in fear. He hugged me close, and I wrapped my arms around his waist.

"Everything is going to be ok," he whispered. I worried Rosswick would get worse before he returned, but I nodded. He let me go and ran off, leaving me nervous and apprehensive. I stood there for a moment, wondering what was going through Zane's head. He had fascinated me since the moment we met, and I had grown quite fond of him. Remembering Rosswick, I looked down. He was gargling on his own blood. I dropped to my knees beside him and lifted his head up. He seemed to do better in an upright position. I put one of his arms over my shoulder as I struggled to carry him into the church. He was groaning as I dragged him inside.

Once in, I sat him down on a bench and kept him in an upright position. Rosswick seemed to be going into shock as he kept shaking intensely. I found some blankets piled next to the door and placed a few around him to keep him upright. When I placed a blanket over him, he seemed to relax for the moment. I wondered how a minister was going to make all of his wounds better. He needed a doctor, stitches, and maybe even a blood transfusion.

I looked around for anything to block the door with, but everything seemed to be nailed to the floor. I heard slamming noises coming from the cellar once again, and I knew I didn't have much time left before the cellar door would give out. I looked up towards the ceiling and noticed some loose chairs stacked in the chancel. I saw a ladder and quickly began to climb up and look around. I grabbed a couple chairs and dropped them to the first floor.

I heard a loud smash come from below. I knew immediately that the super wolves had gotten out and were making their way into the church. I feared that Rosswick was going to be torn to shreds. Hiding up top, I looked down and saw them flood into the sanctuary. Rosswick was unconscious on the bench still, but they didn't seem to bother with him. It was as if they were looking for something else now. All I could do was hope Rosswick remained safe.

16

SAVE ROSSWICK

Later, Zane told me about his frightful mission to save his best friend, and how it began with trying to locate David the minister. On the race to the school, he had to pass through a group of ghouls. He zoomed by, and they didn't seem to notice him at all. Using the *Zumada* spell, he ran so fast that they thought he was just the wind. The ghouls were startled for a moment as they frantically ran in circles when they smelled Zane. Chuckling at the ghouls, Zane walked up to the school and reached out for the handle. To his surprise, the door was unlocked, and he was able to walk right in. The halls were quiet, and the lights were dim. He scoured the halls in search of David, but to no avail.

He crept towards some noises he heard coming from the far side of one hall. There was an enormous man holding a giant mallet—it was a gorgon. He was the size of an ogre, with chains hanging from his arms and waist. He must have weighed four or five hundred pounds and was wearing shorts and a shirt full of holes and torn at his shoulder. It didn't appear to be the exact one he had seen in his vision from the police station. The stench was almost unbearable, a mix of rotting flesh and strong body odor. The gorgon swung his homemade-looking mallet, crumbling lockers around him. A large pole or tree made the mallet's handle while a spiked stone made up the head, all wrapped together with a black material of some sort.

That was all Zane was able to see before the gorgon started to act suspicious, like he could smell him. Stricken with fear, Zane froze against the wall on the other side of the hall, just out of sight. He glanced around, knowing he needed to hide quickly before it found him. Gorgons were dangerous creatures to encounter alone. They hunted primarily by scent and sound, tracking down those who possessed magic and shredding them to pieces. Zane quietly opened a classroom door and snuck in without being discovered.

Once in the room, he closed the door quietly behind him. Zane turned around with a sigh of relief and to his surprise saw David hiding in there too. The minister was extremely shaken up, and his entire left arm was smashed and shredded. It looked like he had run his arm through a printing press. Zane rushed over to assist him with his arm. He quickly took off his belt to make a tourniquet close to his shoulder.

"How are you?" Zane asked.

"I'm in a lot of pain, but I'm just glad to still be alive," David mumbled.

He stayed on the floor with his back against the wall below some windows that were across from the door.

"Why did you come for me?" he asked Zane.

"We got attacked by a pack of super wolves, and Rosswick got hurt, bad. I know you're a damn good healer. Rosswick said you can heal anything as long as the person is still alive. We need your help to save him."

"I can't do much with my arm like this, and my powers have never let me heal myself, but I will try," David promised. "I've known Rosswick since he was a child growing up here, and I'll do anything to help him."

Zane looked around and saw an emergency escape latch on one of the windows near the corner of the room. He pulled up on the handle to open it. The school's alarm started to sound. Quickly, Zane slipped out the window just as the classroom door swung open and the gorgon came into the room. David was halfway out of the window when the gorgon threw its enormous mallet, striking David in the legs. He screamed in pain as Zane reached in and yanked him the rest of the way out the window. He tossed David over his back and ran away from the school as fast as he could.

Zane ran to the closest building, the gas station where he was going to meet us if Rosswick was up for moving.

"I can't go any further," David gasped. "Leave me here and go find your friends."

"I can't leave you here. If the gorgon comes back, you won't stand a chance."

They waited awhile, Zane pacing back and forth impatiently. Fearing the worst, Zane felt he needed to go back to the church to check on us.

"Go quickly," David told Zane. He took a large stick and staggered over to a chair inside the station. Zane was hesitant to leave him alone and helped him get inside.

"Go, I'll be fine," David yelled.

"I'll be quick" Zane replied as he left in a hurry to head back to the church.

~~~~~~

As the wolves circled the church below me, I could only hope Zane would come back to get us soon. My heart leapt as someone kicked in the front doors, only to realize it wasn't Zane, but the bar owner Charley, holding a machine gun, and Veronica, the girl with wings.

Charley opened fire on the super wolves as Veronica quickly flew up to me and shot down at the wolves. Veronica kept shooting, missing, and almost hitting Rosswick with her terrible aim.

"Be careful" I yelled at her. She was so focused on the moving wolves, she wasn't listening. I thought quickly and looked around before casting the Encanto spell to make a small hole through the wall next to me so we could escape. The spell worked, destroying about two feet of wall. I was too close to the blast, and it sent debris flying back at me, covering me in little cuts that burned from the insulation in the wall. I managed to kick out the rest of the hanging debris from the hole to escape.

"Hurry up!" Charley yelled at us. "Get out! I can't hold them off much longer."

The two super wolves that were left were trying to figure out how to get up to us.

I looked down at Rosswick one last time before escaping through the hole. I feared for his safety, and I knew I couldn't go down and get him. There was no way I could even carry him up. Zane suddenly rushed in at just the right moment. It was as if he read my mind. He picked Rosswick up and ran out with him, using his quick speed. I was so relieved that he had come back for us. I crawled through the hole and climbed down the side of the church. Holding onto the ledges, I made it over to a gutter and slid down to the ground from there.

I crept around to the front of the church where I met up with Rosswick and Zane. Veronica and Charley were still inside, but we had to go. Rosswick was bleeding profusely, and he needed help desperately. We had to leave them or Rosswick was going to die. I could see that Zane was visibly tired and needed help carrying Rosswick. We both grabbed an arm and leg and tried to walk as quickly as we could. Zane and I carried Rosswick to the gas station, where David was waiting. By the time we arrived, Zane was extremely exhausted and needed to rest. His powers were drained, and he was worn out from the running.

We laid Rosswick down as David struggled to get over to him. He raised one arm over Rosswick and tried his hardest to heal him. Struggling with one arm, David continued to exert all of his energy over Rosswick. David began to cry as he hovered above him. Suddenly his fingertips illuminated with a golden glow, casting light over Rosswick's nearly lifeless body. It appeared to be working. Rosswick started to wake. The minister began to shake and turn pale. Barely conscious, David fell back. I could see he was dying and had given his last bit of energy to save Rosswick.

"Don't let them get the book," he muttered with his dying breathe. I held him up.

"Don't let who get what book?" I asked, but he was already gone. I felt an abundance of emotions. I was confused, scared, and overwhelmed. I began to weep while I laid him back down, trying to wake him. I'd never seen someone die in front of me before. I placed my jacket over top of him before Rosswick noticed. Rosswick was awake but groggy and saw what David had done for him. Rosswick dragged himself over to his lifeless body, pulled the jacket off, and mumbled a prayer for him.

"Why would you do this?" Rosswick cried out to David.

"He was dying anyway," Zane said as he held his friend.

I walked over to comfort Rosswick as Zane began going through David's pockets. He found a small flat locket and a thin book. The locket was a small box with lines running across the top vertically on a gold chain. I opened the locket and tears fell down my face as I saw the minister with his wife and son. They were laughing in the photo, a time when he was happy. I looked up at the guys and closed the locket. I gave it to Rosswick, who put it back with David's body. He wrapped his hand around the locket and placed his arm over his chest to keep it near his heart. Zane opened the book... but there were only empty pages. He handed it to Rosswick, who was able to see the words written inside the small book. It was an enchanted book.

"It's his prayer book," Rosswick said. Only a few gifted people could read from it. That's when I found out that David was Rosswick's uncle.

It troubled me to leave David's body there, but I knew we had to leave. "We need to go find Jane," I said.

"You need to cast the *Amoranora* spell to find her," Zane said, looking at me.

It was the spell I struggled with the most. Zane talked me through the spell while I cast it. I started to see that Jane was in a house. It was a house I had passed before, and I remembered where it was. Rosswick was still recovering, so he wouldn't be able to go yet.

"I need to stay with Rosswick until he's better and able to move around more," Zane said, still exhausted. I watched Rosswick stagger over to a chair. "Go, Anya. It shouldn't be too far away."

I hesitantly agreed and left alone, frightened of what horrifying events might lie ahead. Bad luck seemed to follow me, and I feared what might happen without the guys, but I left anyway.

17

A SPECIAL BOOK

Wandering street after street, searching for the house I had seen in my vision, I finally saw Jane. She was slowly walking backwards into the street away from the house with a look of fear. I walked up to her and looked at the house where she was looking but didn't see anything. I went to speak when she looked at me.

"Where are the others?" she asked in a strange, panicked tone.

"They're waiting for us to meet them back at the gas station," I said. "We need to get out of this place, but we can't leave without you." I was still shaken up as I told her everything that had been happening.

"As long as you help me first, we can go" she replied.

She ran back to the porch that she was suspiciously walking away from and began to drag a long heavy duffle bag down the driveway. I was afraid it was a body by the way she was acting. When I questioned her, she told me the bags were full of money for Seth and the mansion. She had a look of concern when she said it though.

"Why do we need all this money?" I asked.

"If I don't get it back to Seth, he'll kill me," she said.

I was shocked and confused about what we were really doing. Seth wouldn't kill her over money—he was rich and had lots of money. Why and how would he even know where to get money out of this place? And if he did know how to get money out, why hadn't he come for us yet? I had so many questions.

"Ok, ok listen to me, Anya. Things aren't what they seem at the mansion," Jane said in distress. "Seth sends me and Eddy on missions a lot of the time to handle his shady deals. He makes us swear to never tell the others or anyone about it."

"What?" I asked, surprised at what she was saying. However, Jane didn't want to explain any further. She acted like she was afraid to even talk about it.

"Anya, when we get out of this place, we should go. We should run away," she said, terrified.

"What's going on with you, Jane" I asked, confused.

"There are some things you just don't know yet. Are you in or not?" she pleaded.

"I can't do that. I can't do it to the guys, my biological parents, or my mom," I said as I worried about her. "We can't just run away."

"Fine," she said with anger. "Let's just go. Please promise me you won't tell ANYONE about this."

"Promise, now can we go?" I shouted. I couldn't handle this right now—Seth was our only way out of here, and if he really was as bad as Jane was saying, we had no hope and the entire last year of my life had been a lie. As she walked back to the house, all I could think about was what Seth really wanted me for or if he was really trying to help me.

Lost in my thoughts, I helped Jane load up a truck she had parked in front of the house. There were five large bags that we had to drag across the front lawn. Once we had grabbed everything, we drove down the road slowly, fearful of what we might come across. We followed what she said were Seth's directions and dropped the truck off at that location. It was in the back of a parking lot on the far side of town, across from where the post office was. Walking back, Jane began to open up to me.

"You remember when you asked me what my special gift was?" she said calmly.

"Yes," I replied with a questionable glare at her.

"I'm actually a myotonic vulpes, a sort of shape shifter. I can turn into a fox."

I stared at her intensely for a moment before responding. It all was making sense to me now. "I knew I wasn't crazy. I swore I saw something with a furry tail run through the kitchen at that one house I found you in. How long have you been able to shift? That's how you're able to hide so well and scare me so easily all the time," I shouted at her in excitement.

"Anya, you can't tell the guys about any of this," Jane said.

"Why don't you want them to know?" I questioned, but she got visibly frustrated with me.

"NEVER TELL ANYONE ABOUT THIS EVER," she shouted.

"Ok, calm down," I said.

We continued to walk in silence back to the gas station where Zane and Rosswick were waiting. We kept hearing noises all around us, but it was so dark outside we couldn't see if something was following us or not.

Once we arrived at the gas station, we discovered the guys were gone.

"I can find them with the spell I placed on Zane," Jane said excitedly.

"Why would you put on a spell on Zane?" I asked, looking at her in surprise.

She shrugged. "Because I can," she replied.

I wanted to argue with her because she knew I liked him, but she started casting a spell that I had never seen before. She poured some special stones out of her bag and lined them up in a circle. Jane whispered some words and spun her hand over the stones until a glow appeared. She was able to locate him like a tracking device. She looked up at me.

"He's at the other church in town." It was a little ways up from where we were, and I was glad she knew how to find it.

We began to walk towards the outskirts of town where the church was. We walked quite a ways, and I was losing hope that she knew where it was. Then, to my surprise, she led us straight to it. This church was only a single-story building but very old and unique. It had large stone walls with wooden logs making up some parts around the windows and corners. The entrance was on the side of the building and had two large pillars holding up an overhang. There were two solid wood doors with iron brackets and a door knocker on the left side. I had an ominous feeling as I approached the doors. They were shut, and the area was quiet. Jane suggested we just go in, but after several failed attempts, the doors were too heavy for me to open myself, so Jane came over to help me. We still weren't able to open it. We started to yell for the guys or anyone inside, and the doors began to creak loudly.

It was Rosswick struggling to open them, pushing slowly. Zane was lying inside, nearly passed out. He was still so exhausted from earlier and hadn't fully recovered from all the running and lack of sleep. I went over to his side to make sure he was ok.

"I'm fine," he assured me. "I just need to rest for a while." We all decided to stay at the church and try to take it easy till Zane recovered. After an hour or two of relaxing, we raided the church kitchen. Rosswick hadn't eaten with us earlier, so he got some food first and brought some over to Zane. Jane kept pacing back and forth. She just wanted to leave the church and look for a way out of this place already.

Jane finally calmed down and came over to sit with us. We told the guys about the noises we heard when we were walking to meet them at the gas station.

"We were hearing the same sounds around the gas station too," Rosswick said. "That's why we left and went up town to get away from whatever was coming. I remembered this church, hidden on the outskirts of town. Some friends of mine would skateboard here when we were younger."

I could tell by his facial expressions he had good memories here.

"When they showed me this place, we would spend hours skateboarding all over here, doing tricks from the front handicap ramp." Rosswick began to stare off, lost in his memories.

"What happened to you? Why did you leave this place?" I asked as his happy smile turned to sadness.

"It wasn't a popular church," he said, ignoring my question, "because it was kind of far out of town." He wasn't wrong—it sat so far back from the main road many people probably didn't even know it existed.

I could tell my question struck a nerve. I wondered what really happened to him here, but I knew I couldn't ask again. "What do you think David meant when he said to protect the book?"

"It's probably something special he hid somewhere no one would ever look" Rosswick replied, more accepting of this question.

"What's so special about a book?" I asked, but he just shrugged.

"I'm not sure why David even mentioned a book," he said.

Out of nowhere, the heavy door flung open, making me to jump from my seat. It was Eddy, and he looked like a mess. His clothes were torn, and he had a large gash on his arm that was bleeding. He was so covered in mud and ash he barely looked like himself. He came in and sat on the other side of Zane. That's when I noticed he had other smaller cuts all over his face and arms.

"What are you doing here?" Eddy asked.

I told him we needed to find some kind of special book.

"What book?" he asked. "Rosswick and I saw a magical book earlier when we were hiding in a house up in the hills."

"I'm not sure what it's supposed to look like, but I believe it can help us get out of this realm," I told him.

We all agreed we should at least go check it out.

I got up and walked over to Jane.

"Can you find us a ride since you abandoned our car at the police station?" I asked her.

"Wait here. I'll be right back," she said as she jumped up with excitement.

I waited, talking to Eddy for a few minutes to find out what happened to him.

"I found my items," he said with excitement. "I also found some other cool pieces special to this realm."

"Where in this hellhole did you find them?" I asked, surprised. "Your thief was killed. How would you even know where to begin?"

"Well, after being chased deep into the forest, I stumbled across what I thought was shelter, a cave that was full of treasures," Eddy said excitedly.

I was happy for him as I could see the relief on his face.

"At least the trip wasn't a total waste," he chuckled.

A few moments later, we heard a loud rumbling sound. Rosswick opened the door, and it turned out to be Jane pulling into the parking lot. She had brought back a four-wheeler. I wanted to ask her where she had found it in such a small town, but I was so excited to drive it I didn't care where she found it. I remembered as a child riding a small four-wheeler that made traveling so much fun. I quickly hopped onto it and looked back at Eddy, who was now standing in the doorway ready to go.

"It would be better if Rosswick goes so you can rest," I told Eddy. "Jane can clean your cuts."

Jane liked Eddy, so she quickly began to drag him back inside. I really didn't want Jane to go either, since she was bound to stir up trouble, and Rosswick knew where this place was.

"Come on, Rosswick," I yelled.

"No, I'm driving!" he shouted.

"Just get on already," I begged him. He huffed in annoyance and rolled his eyes, but finally got on behind me.

"You only have one chance before I'm taking over," he said. I laughed and nodded at him before turning the four-wheeler on and driving away.

18

SAVIORS OR TRICKS

We had just started our drive north up the hill when we noticed Charley following behind us with his motorcycle rumbling loudly. He sped up alongside us.

"I saw Jane riding through town, and figured she needed help with something," he shouted. I smiled at him, thinking we could use the extra fire power in case we ran into anything. I pulled over so we could talk to him. Rosswick got off first and walked over to him as he turned his bike off. I could hear them chatting faintly as I turned our machine off and walked over to join them.

"Thanks, man, for saving us. I don't know if I'd be here without you guys," Rosswick said, shaking his hand.

I looked around for a moment before asking, "Hey, where's Veronica?"

Charley looked at me with tear-filled eyes. "They got her."

Shocked by his response, I quickly asked, "What got her?" fearing the wolves had torn her to pieces.

"The realm keepers came and took her once we escaped the church. She will face her charges in her realm for the crimes she has committed. I know you guys are the key out of here so I can save her." he cried out.

"Realm keepers came here? How did they get in and out? Why aren't they helping us?" I shouted in anger.

"Realm keepers only intervene when absolutely necessary. They were always opposed to this realm anyway. And they can come and go through any realm whenever they want. They don't need a gateway to do it," Rosswick tried to explain.

"I'll do anything to help you guys get this gate back open," Charley said with anger in his eyes.

"Hell, yeah, man, let's go then," Rosswick yelled. We continued riding along the dark winding road as fast as we could, Charley right behind us the whole time. We traveled deep into the mountains with only our headlights and some moonlight to see.

Dark patches seemed to flicker in the moonlight. Strikers, casting shadows, flew over us by the dozens and seemed to follow us in the night sky. We could only make out glimpses of them flying over us. We sped up, weaving through the woods trying to lose them.

Rosswick leaned forward to say the house was close, but I couldn't see anything but trees and about ten feet of headlights in front of us.

"The house goes invisible and changes appearance, so it's hard to find," he shouted.

"How did you find it to begin with?" I replied.

He went to respond, but before he could, we smashed into an invisible wall. On impact, the four-wheeler's rear end lifted, crushing Rosswick and I like a sandwich into the side of the house. The house flickered for a moment as if it had a short in its magical shield and suddenly appeared clear as day. Charley pulled up and came to a stop.

"Found it!" he yelled, laughing.

Rosswick and I fell off the four-wheeler as it slammed back to the ground. I stood up, a bit dazed, and noticed I was bleeding from my arm. It was a minor scrape compared to everything else I had gone through. I helped Rosswick get up on his feet. I pointed out that he had split his bottom lip. I looked over at Charley.

"Thanks for the help," I yelled in anger as I brushed myself off. Rosswick and I stood at the bottom step to the house. "You coming or what?" I shouted at Charley. He didn't want to go in though.

"I'll wait for you guys out here," he replied as he sat against his bike. I walked up the steps first and Rosswick followed close behind. The moon's light lit up the night sky and cast a shadow over the porch to the door. I tugged on the handle, but the door wouldn't open. It couldn't have been locked since I was able to turn the knob freely. I casted the *Encanto* spell, not knowing what it would do to the door. The blast blew a hole through the door and burned most of the floor and furniture inside.

After the smoke cleared and the debris settled, Rosswick dashed in and saw a large brown book sitting on top of a pedestal, with a strange red glow coming from its core. It was the only thing near the entryway that wasn't burnt. The book didn't even have a mark or any debris on it like everything else. He went to pick it up, but the book started to dissolve around his hands. He watched it fall through his fingers like sand and turned to look at me, confused. We rushed back to the porch when we noticed the sky light up like a flash of lightening frozen in time. I started to get that strange feeling again as I tugged on Rosswick's arm. I turned to look at him, only to see his eyes were glowing red. I backed down the steps away from him in shock.

"What's wrong?" he asked.

I tried to tell him about his eyes, but the wind picked up and swirled my hair into my face. Leaves and limbs were blowing all around us. Rosswick began to freak out, yelling that my eyes were red. I thought he was trying to cover for himself and turn it around on me. I didn't know what he was becoming, but he wasn't Rosswick anymore. Something was possessing him. I looked over to see Charley near his bike, looking confused. Rosswick kept calling me a monster, but I saw him as the threat while he kept circling me. I didn't know what was going on, and in a panic, I began to look around for an escape route.

Trees began to lift themselves from the ground and move as they swayed back and forth from the wind, reaching out to grab at us. Rosswick pulled out a knife and swung it at me. I pulled out my katana and held it against his blade. As we fought each other, the woods around us came to life and began to attack us. A large branch knocked me back as Rosswick tried to stab me. When one came towards me again, I quickly rolled to dash away from it. Rosswick swung at me again but missed, striking the four-wheeler. I got up and yelled for him to stop, but he wouldn't listen. I jumped on the four-wheeler but couldn't get it to turn on. Rosswick had destroyed the ignition when he stabbed it. Then his attention turned towards Charley. I shook the key in the ignition to try and get it to start while he seemed distracted.

Suddenly, Rosswick charged towards Charley. I jumped off the four-wheeler and ran after him to stop him. I knew he was going to leave me here. As we ran, Charley pulled out two double-barreled revolvers and aimed at each of us. We both froze as he looked at us.

"Only one of you can fit on my bike," he said. "Or I'll leave both of you dead where you lie." We looked at each other and were about to fight for it when something else began to happen.

I saw a monster that looked like a small hobbit walk out from the woods. I wasn't sure what it was as I stared. The monster was greenish brown, covered in hair, with large brown eyes. It appeared to be wearing moss like a coat and stood only about knee high. Looking up at me with its big, adorable eyes, it quickly pulled out a small dagger and began stabbing at my calves. I tried to kick at it, but my kicks went right through it. I panicked as there was nothing I could do to keep it away.

"Help me!" I yelled at Rosswick and Charley as I jumped around trying to get away. I cast an invisibility spell to cloak myself as I ran towards the motorcycle.

"Look! You can see her footsteps," Rosswick yelled to Charley. Charley blocked my path to his bike.

"No more tricks, witch," Charley shouted. I looked back to see the gremlin still chasing after me as I turned towards the woods and continued running. I didn't know where I was going, but I kept running through the dark forest trying to get away.

It continued chasing me, and I knew if I stopped running, it was going to kill me. It managed to stab me a few more times in my arms and shoulder as it swung through the trees. I looked at my arm and could see blood pouring from my shoulder. I cried out in pain as I ran deep into the forest. The little monster was swinging from the trees, and I didn't know what to do. I wondered why I was the only one who saw it and why it was only chasing me.

Running through some thick brush, I didn't see the cliff's edge coming up and fell down it. I rolled and tumbled until I reached the bottom. I laid there looking up at the night sky for several minutes. Glancing around, it appeared I was in a small canyon shaped like a fishbowl. I was now banged and bruised everywhere from old and new wounds, but I knew I couldn't stop running. I managed to pull myself up and realized I had a sharp pain in my ankle. I tried to keep running until I just couldn't bear the pain anymore.

I looked around for a place to hide and found a spot behind some shrubs in a ditch with a fallen tree hanging over it. I sat there and began to cry despite trying to hold back my emotions. Dirty, bleeding, and in immense pain, I wasn't sure what to do next. I tore a piece of my shirt and held it over the gash in my shoulder. I was all alone, lost deep in this mysterious forest. That's when I heard something rustling behind me. I feared the little monster had found me.

To my surprise, it was the little girl from the post office. She was slowly creeping around trees and sniffing at the air like a feral animal. I knew it! She was the little girl from the woods, the demon girl that turned into a wolf and ran off. She wasn't in her noisy armor, but I knew it was her. I stayed very still and tried to hold my breath, but it was no use. She popped around the tree I was hiding behind.

"There you are!" she said in a low-toned voice. I looked at her with confusion and feared what she was going to do.

"I'm not going to hurt you," she said. "I'm here to save you."

"Save me from what?" I asked, confused.

"The tortui," she whispered, looking over her shoulder, then back at me.

"Is that what's chasing me?"

"Tortuis are demons that seek out the most powerful people," she explained. "They usually hunt in packs of three to five, but this one is traveling alone, which means he broke their code of rules for some reason."

"What code of rules?" I asked, pissed. "That thing is out to kill me!"

She kept looking over her shoulder and got closer to me before continuing. "They have rules they must obey in order to maintain their magic and not be destroyed by the elders. Their first rule is to never break into other realms, but they are given permission and gate keys to enter for specific reasons. The second rule says that they aren't allowed to attack mage minors or parents with their minors present. You are clearly still a minor, and that breaks their rule. Their third and final rule says that they have to have a written order to kill specific mages. This tortui is not with a pack and broke the realm gateway to enter this realm and attack a minor. You must be one powerful person for it to break all the rules they live by."

"Why would it think I'm a powerful mage? I can barely control my powers," I asked, confused.

"No, I'm telling you, you're more than just that. The tortui knows it too," she quickly replied.

"Why are you helping me? Why don't you just kill me?" I asked.

"My father and I are looking to stop the tortui because they broke the law and must be punished."

"But I overheard your father telling the ghouls to kill everyone with magic," I said.

"We try to capture mages and interrogate them to make sure they aren't breaking any laws and telling norms," she replied. "We don't kill them."

"Norms?" I asked.

"Non-magical people," she said. "Most of our people moved to this realm a few months ago to escape the horror of our new leader, Jarbin. He overthrew my father, and we barely made it out alive with some of our people. We got trapped in this realm recently. That's when we guessed the tortui was chasing someone and broke the gateway."

She stared at me for a moment before leaning over me, putting her hands on my temples. "Let me show you something," she said.

19

THE CHOSEN ONE

Flashes of light took over my sight, and before I could push her back, I was sucked into a vision. She brought me to a place in her mind, a bright sunny meadow with lots of wildflowers as far as I could see. Sound was muffled and the wind was blowing when she reached out and grabbed my hand. She pulled me through the flowers until we reached the end of the meadow. She looked at me and held my hand tightly as we walked through a dark, creepy forest. The farther we walked, the more things began to change. The sky became dark, and the trees were dying or dead. A short while later, we walked out into what looked like a valley of death. Everything was now dark and gloomy, and the sky was grey with a tinge of red. A frigid gust of wind blew by and sent chills down my spine. She looked up at me, pulling me over to the cliff's edge and pointing down. Looking below, I could see people chipping away at stones with primitive tools.

"Where are we?" I asked. Sound still seemed to be muffled in this vision. "What are they doing?"

"It's a demon's prison. This is who has your parents," she said. "His name is Jarbin. He's the new leader of the wolf demons, not my father."

"Why are you showing me all of this?" I asked.

"My father was exiled for his friendship with the gifted people. For his friendship with your father. Jarbin grew angry and felt my father should not befriend the mage. When Jarbin took over, he broke all the rules and enslaved those he wasn't supposed to, your parents included. I've heard legends of your existence. Your parents are leaders of a rebel cult group. The story says they hid you in the real world, where crooked demons wouldn't find you. When I spotted you here, I knew you were the one. I knew that if you had half the powers your parents have then you could save them. You can save all of us from the rule of Jarbin."

I frantically tried to find a way down to save these people, but the little girl stopped me.

"You can't save these slaves," she said. "This is just a memory you're seeing, not how it is now."

"Please, get me out of here," I begged, grabbing her arm. Seeing those people enraged me, and I felt a surge through my body that I had never felt before. Rage-driven, I knew it wasn't good. She just stared at me like she wanted to say something.

"We're trapped, unable to exit this realm without the book to open the gate," she said sadly, looking down.

"We need to find my friends," I said. "We can all work together to get out of here."

"Deal!" she cried, sticking out her hand. "You help us get out of this realm, and we'll help you free the slaves and hopefully get my father back in charge.

"And free my parents!" I said, shaking her hand.

She ended the vision, warping us back to reality where we were still lost in the forest.

"My name is Dalia," she quietly whispered.

"It's nice to finally meet the real you," I said. She smiled back at me.

"Hold still," she said, pulling out some rope. Confused, I hesitantly pulled away from her.

"We need to make a tourniquet for your arm to stop the bleeding till we can stitch it."

I felt foolish and allowed her to tie the rope tight around my arm to stop the bleeding. She then patrolled the area to see if there was an easy escape route. Once she returned, she said it was clear all the way to her father's camp.

"Your father's camp?" I asked hesitantly. "Is it safe for me?"

She laughed. "Yes, let's go."

Following her, I kept looking back as we quietly ran through the woods towards the camp, stopping frequently to rest my ankle. Some ways down, we finally reached the edge of the forest and her father's campsite. I could see tepee style tents everywhere. Wolves and people wandering all around stared at us entering the camp. Dalia held my hand as she pulled me through the village of tents. I could see and hear people whispering and muttering words to one another, but I wasn't able to make out what they were saying. We finally made it to the center tent, which had markings and bright colors painted onto it. I wondered who Dalia had brought me too until suddenly I saw him: the man from the forest who ordered the hunt of magical people. I was frozen with fear as I watched him walk up to us slowly.

"Father," Dalia said quickly. He put his hand up, stopping her from continuing.

"Why would you bring her to our camp?" he asked, looking at me then back to Dalia. She bowed to him before answering, and I did the same.

"We agreed to help one another. I saved her from a tortui, and she knows where the book is."

He turned to me, grabbing both of my arms, pulling me close to him. "You know where the book is?" he shouted. "Where is it?"

"My friends and I were getting what we thought was it before we were attacked by the gremlin thing," I said, stricken with fear and pain. He let me go as he laughed with a deep horrifying voice, looking down at Dalia.

"You're now responsible for her," he said, and turned to walk away. As others watched the spectacle, Dalia grabbed my hand and turned to her father.

"When we get the key and get out of this realm, I promised Anya we would free the slaves Jarbin took and save her parents."

Angry, he snarled and turned back towards us. My eyes widened, and I felt my heart beating.

"How could you make such a deal knowing that we cannot defeat Jarbin?" he screamed at her. Dalia walked over to him calmly.

"She is more powerful than she knows, Father. She can help us defeat Jarbin."

He stared in anger at her before shouting "She doesn't even know what she is! How is this girl going to help us, Dalia? She will fail and surely be the end of us all."

"Father, I know she's the one. I've seen it. Please let me try."

Her father nodded in disappointment before telling us to go and find my friends and bring them back here.

Dalia brought me over to a tent and said she would have someone put stitches in my shoulder. I trembled with fear. I had never had stitches before and couldn't imagine how bad they would feel. She waved over another woman who had come in behind us. Dalia introduced me to Magpen. She was their healer, or shamanka, as Dalia called her. She was a very old woman with white hair in many knots, with sticks and feathers hanging from it. She had a lot of piercings on her face and wore baggy clothes.

"Can you stitch her arm?" Dalia asked, looking at Magpen. Magpen never said anything, just looked at Dalia and nodded her head slowly before she walked away.

"She'll be back," Dalia said, while she washed my arm around my wound. When Magpen returned with a bag of supplies, I began to shake in fear.

"Is this going to hurt?" I asked Dalia.

"It will pinch a little," she said, as she gave me a piece of leather to bite onto. I quickly put the piece into my mouth as the shamanka poured something over the wound that burned. As I shrieked in pain, she began to sew up my arm, and I looked away. I felt a pinch and tugging with every stitch.

"The bleeding has stopped. You're good," Dalia said as Magpen finished. She untied the rope around my arm, and I spit out the leather and sighed in relief. I flexed my fingers, which were partially numb from the tourniquet.

"Just a little pinch, huh?" I said, looking at her.

She laughed. "Let's go find your friends."

Everyone stared at me again as I walked out of the camp, limping. Dalia said we were near town and just had to pass along a small trail up ahead to get back near the gas station. That's when I remembered the noises Jane and I had heard near it earlier. They were probably coming from her people at their camp site.

"This has felt like the longest night ever," I sighed.

"It's the longest night I have seen so far in this realm. The tortui that broke the realm gateway has cursed this place in search of you," she said. As she spoke, I wondered how it could be me. I didn't want to talk about it anymore, though. I just wanted to get out of this nightmare.

"My friends are nearby, in the church past the gas station," I said. She motioned for me to lead the way.

Walking through the parking lot of the church, I saw the lights still on inside. I figured it was a good sign that they were still there. I cautiously walked up to the door, and Zane saw me coming and opened it. He stood in the doorway, blocking the entrance, and asked what happened. I told him about Rosswick, the book, and how his eyes changed.

"What happened to you?" he asked.

"Are you going to let us in so I can explain everything?"

"Why did you run away?" Zane asked.

"I was being attacked," I said, but Zane acted like he didn't believe me.

"It's all true," Dalia said. "She was attacked by a creature called a tortui.

Zane seemed surprised by that and relieved to hear that I wasn't turning into some sort of monster. He let us in, and I had to explain everything to the others. After telling everyone what happened, I asked where Rosswick was.

Zane pulled me aside and explained what Rosswick said happened after I ran away through the woods. He and Charley were left confused and began to fight with one another. During their scuffle, Rosswick was shot in the abdomen but managed to get the gun away and kill Charley. When Rosswick returned on Charley's motorcycle, he was barely conscious. I was shocked to hear what happened. Rosswick was Zane's best friend, and we'd already been through so much to save him.

"The house must have been a trap," Zane said. "You guys must've been under some sort of spell after touching the book. It made you both see each other as something evil."

"I want to see Rosswick and apologize," I said.

"He's resting." Zane stopped me quickly. "I just removed the bullet and bandaged him up."

I felt so bad about what happened. If I hadn't run away, I could have helped him. Zane pulled me close and hugged me. I wrapped my arms around him and kept telling him I was so sorry; I shouldn't have left Rosswick. Zane assured me Rosswick should be ok, but I knew that was just him trying to convince himself.

We remained at the church for several hours while Rosswick rested and waited for morning to come. Zane was concerned about moving him, especially at night, until we could get him out of here and to a hospital. I agreed but said that we still needed the book. Dalia said she was going to run back to camp to tell her father what was going on and why we hadn't returned. After she left, I tried to brainstorm with the others to try and figure out why the book melted.

"Maybe we've seen the book already but didn't know it," Eddy said, joining the conversation. That's when Zane stared off with a vexed look on his face.

"I had the book!" Zane said. "I had it at the police barracks when we first arrived!"

I looked at him, confused.

"It all makes sense now," he continued. "Remember when we first arrived, and we noticed something strange was going on around town? The gateway we used to get in closed and wouldn't open again." I nodded hesitantly.

"Remember how we went to the police station, and I saw an officer in my vision who brought in a box with random items before some beast busted in? What if they weren't after the police but the stuff in the box that they had just brought into evidence?"

Ok, this was making a little more sense than our other theory that the attacks were random. Zane stood up and began to pace back and forth thinking.

"What did you do with the box?" I asked.

Zane froze and looked at me. "I put it in the truck before we went to look for the creature." He turned to Jane.

"Is the truck still there?" Before Jane could answer, I pulled my backpack off.

"I have it," I quietly said. "I took it from the box when we were waiting for you guys." I couldn't believe I had it the whole time.

"How could you have the book this whole time and be so stupid to not realize it?" Jane yelled, clearly upset at me.

"I put it in my bag before the ghouls attacked and forgot about it, ok?" I shouted back. "I didn't have it long enough to even remember, so back off." Zane looked surprised and impressed by my anger. He came over to me.

"Can I see the book?" he asked. I pulled it out and it began to shimmer in my hands. As I handed it to Zane, its shimmer faded, and it soon looked like an ordinary old book. He flipped it over but couldn't figure out how it opened. It had a combination lock with a metal bracket wrapped around it. He tried to use his crypto key, but it wouldn't work on the book since there was no keyhole for it to go in. As he handed it back to me, the book began to shimmer once again. Confused, he pulled it back towards himself and watched the shimmer dull out.

"I think the book likes you," he said jokingly. Then he held the book near me and watched it began to shimmer again.

Jane, who was still aggravated, came over and snatched the book from Zane's hand, trying to pry it open. Suddenly a large spark came from the book, sending Jane flying across the room.

"There must be some sort of protection spell preventing others from breaking into the book," he said. At that moment, Rosswick came stumbling out from the back area of the church where he was resting. Eddy darted over to him to help hold him upright as I ran to check on Jane.

"The book is a scrumpage," Rosswick said.

"A what?" we all asked.

"The book holds the key to get out of this realm," he continued. "But it chooses who is worthy to possess the power of gate keeper."

"So, you're saying the book chose Anya?" Zane asked, walking over to stand near Rosswick. I helped Jane to her feet and moved some broken chairs away from her. I couldn't help but wonder why the book would choose me. Rosswick began coughing and holding his abdomen in pain as Eddy and Zane led him to a bench.

"Why do you think it chose me?" I asked, walking over to him. He began to cough up a little blood.

"It's always been you. You're the chosen one to restore balance in this realm. It was always your destiny."

"How do you know that?" Eddy asked as he applied pressure to Rosswick's abdomen.

"The realms only choose one person to take control in times like this. The scrumpage is an item that finds its way to a person of its choosing." Coughing excessively, he continued. "Anya found herself in possession of it this entire time. The attacks that seemed to be isolated to her are because other creatures are drawn to the aura it puts off."

I hesitantly looked around at the others in surprise. "What am I supposed to do?" I asked, but Rosswick shook his head as if he was unsure.

"Hold on to the book and bring it to the gateway," he muttered with blood smudged on his chin. "It will reveal what you need to do there."

Things began to make sense now. That must have been why everything seemed to be attacking me and not the others as much. I had the book with me this entire time, and it seemed like every awful monster knew it but us. I knew we had to get to the gateway quickly, before Rosswick got any worse from his wound. I pulled Zane aside.

"What should we do? We can't just wait here forever. Rosswick is only getting worse."

"We need to find a way to the gateway like Rosswick said. It's his only chance." Zane sadly whispered.

"Dalia and her people can help us get safely across town," I said. "I don't know what's taking her so long though."

"It will be ok," Zane replied. "She'll be back soon, and we'll figure out what to do to get Rosswick out of here. Just be patient." He left to change Rosswick's bandages once again. Everyone could see that he was losing a lot of blood through the gauze, so Eddy and Zane carried him to the back.

I went and sat near Jane, who apologized for snapping at me earlier. We began plotting our escape route.

"Do you trust Dalia?" Jane asked.

"I'm not sure," I told her quietly. "But I need to believe that she'll help me free my parents."

"If you trust her, then we will trust her," Jane said, looking at me with a smile. That's when the door opened. It was Dalia and her father.

"The rest of the tribe is outside," Dalia said. "They can move Rosswick."

"I have the book," I said, walking towards them. "We just need to get to the gateway to use it."

I could see the sun was up and dozens of demons were waiting just outside the door. Dalia's father turned towards the door, took a few steps out, and raised his staff to his people.

"We have the key," he cried. "Now march to the gate, protect our gifted friends from anyone who tries to stop them. They are the ones who will help us take back our lands from the treacherous Jarbin."

Crowds of demons began to chant. "Tolsric, Tolsric," they cried. Dalia turned towards me with a smile on her face.

"The people believe in my father again," she said. "Come, let's go now."

"I have to wait," I said. "I need to get Zane and Rosswick." I ran to the back of the church.

Zane was finishing up with Rosswick's wound.

"Hurry!" I told him. "They're waiting for us."

"I heard," Zane said, helping Rosswick stand up.

I put Rosswick's left arm over my shoulder while Zane did the same with his right. We carried him out the door where they had a flat wagon waiting with wolves tethered in leads to pull it. They helped lay Rosswick down, and then we started down the middle of the road, surrounded by other demons to protect him. Tolsric and Dalia led us and the parade of demons behind Rosswick south through the middle of town.

"My father fears the tortui will try and attack before we reach the gate," Dalia said.

I had never felt so safe and scared all at the same time. Zane reached out for my hand and startled me when we touched. I quickly apologized, and Zane looked at me with a big grin on his face.

"Don't be sorry," he said. "I was trying to hold your hand." I could feel my face turning red and butterflies in my stomach as I reached out and held his hand. We continued our journey to the end of town.

20

BROKEN KEY

Nearing the edge of town where the shimmer once was, we all began to gather.

"Hand me the book," Tolsric said as he reached out for it to open the gateway himself.

"It won't work for anyone but me," I said, stopping him.

"Hand me the book," he said again in a low aggressive tone, looking at me in anger.

I held it out to him, and he ripped it from my hands. We watched the glow from the book fade as he held it up with pride for all his people to see. They chanted him on as we watched him struggle to open it. He was about to pry the latch open when Jane stopped him and warned him of the danger she'd experienced trying to open it. He shoved the book back at me and demanded I open it. As I held it, Tolsric noticed the shimmer return to the book. He stepped away from me with a surprised look on his face. I was confused by his actions.

"Do you want me to try to open the gate?" I asked.

"Are you an archmage?" he asked.

I looked over at Zane, confused by what he asked.

I responded by laughing. "A what?"

Dalia quickly jumped in front of her father.

"See I told you, she doesn't know!" she cried. He moved Dalia aside and walked up to me.

"Open the gate," he told me in a stern voice now.

Jane pushed her way back through the crowd to calm me down. "Just give us a moment to figure this out," she told Tolsric calmly. Standing in front of me, she coached me on the words to open the book. I was still not familiar with all of the spells and struggled to pronounce some of the words.

"Repeat what I say," she told me. *"Annuannu Abaca Unlaziala."* I repeated the words while holding the book out in front of me with my palms underneath it. A gust of wind began to swirl and form over the top of the book. I was excited and scared as the wind blew my hair back. A light glowed from the center of the swirl and grew until the book burst open in my hands. The wind began to settle, and I looked out to the people, only to notice they had all moved away from me. I held the book open above my head where it rested in my hand after the wind settled. The tribe began to cheer in excitement. I brought it back down and noticed there was a drawing of the gateway on the left side of the page. This had to be the spell to open the gateway, I thought. I began to speak the words written on the page to the right. After reading the page aloud, nothing seemed to change. Dalia took a few steps towards me.

"What happened?" she asked.

"I'm not sure," I replied.

Looking around, I could see everyone and hear them arguing. But they were fading in and out of sound. I was hyper focusing on some of the people when suddenly I was stricken by a piercing sound in my ears. I fell to the ground in a desperate attempt to cover my ears from the horrific noises. Zane ran over to me trying to pull my arms down from my ears, yelling at me. I could only faintly hear him shouting.

"What's wrong? Anya! What's wrong?"

Falling to my side, I felt like I had passed out, but I could see everything. I laid on the ground with people all around me, unable to make a sound. I felt like I was convulsing when suddenly my body arched, and a beam of light shot out from my mouth like a spotlight. I was no longer in control of anything happening, and I feared I was dying. I could hear people screaming and see some running away. I felt like I was becoming something different, evolving. I began to float up from the ground as my body bent and twisted all around. Something boiled from my core as I reached out for help. I felt my body tearing itself apart from the inside before a growing glow exploded, sending out a blast of light that knocked everyone to the ground.

I dropped from the sky, denting the ground where I knelt. I stood up and brushed myself off, noticing everyone staring back at me. I knew something was wrong, but I had never felt better. I stood there, hair stripped of all its color, eyes as blue as the ocean, with a look that struck fear in everyone. I walked towards the others as a sense took over me.

"I am Anya Emalia Vamour," I said before I could stop myself. "Fifth generation of my people, and now, gatekeeper of Hardgate." I could see Eddy and Jane out in the crowd with their jaws dropped. That's when the shimmer in the gateway reappeared. The gateway was now open. Cheers from the demons rang out as they slowly began to cross to the other side.

Zane walked up from behind, startling me when he ran his fingers through my hair.

"Is it still you?" he asked when I turned to look at him.

"It will always be me," I quickly responded. He smiled. "I just have this overwhelming feeling inside, like a surge of energy that's exciting me."

He laughed and hugged me. "Glad you're ok," he whispered in my ear. "You really freaked me out."

I couldn't help but stare at him with a grin on my face as he walked off. Jane and Eddy ran over to me with excitement, both talking at the same time about how incredible what I had just done was. I had to stop them as I struggled to understand what they were both saying.

"What new powers do you have?" Jane asked me. I laughed because I had no idea.

"We need to hurry and get Rosswick out of here," I told them.

Tolsric and Dalia stopped me to say thanks for freeing them from this realm.

"Don't forget our deal," I reminded them. "I'm keeping my end of it."

"Once we're through that gate and back into your world, we'll be able to find our way back to our realm. We must now travel to our homeland, Valdekka, end the rein of Jarbin once and for all, and take back the land for my people," Tolsric shouted. I reminded them we were going to release all the slaves, including my parents. He nodded as he walked towards the gateway.

Once through to the other side, Rosswick began to spit up more blood. We laid him down on the grass near the road's edge where we could see demons walking away for miles. I looked around in fear for Rosswick. Eddy quickly pointed out a vehicle parked along the road up ahead. It was a large white cargo van. Jane began to walk towards it. We could see her nearing the van when we noticed someone was inside. It was our driver from the house. Seth must have sent him to get us when the gate opened. Jane got in the passenger side, and they drove over to us. We loaded Rosswick in as quickly and carefully as possible.

"How'd you know when the gate was going to open?" Zane asked the driver. The man paused for a moment before looking back at Zane and the rest of us. "I didn't. I've been here waiting for three days." He pointed to the back of the cargo van where there was a sleeping bag and supplies. As the rest of us were getting in, Dalia stopped me.

"We must go now," she said. "We have no time."

"We need to save Rosswick," I said.

"If we don't go now, you won't be able to save your parents," she said. I looked into the van at the others.

"You guys go," I said. "Save Rosswick. I have to finish this!" Zane jumped out.

"I'm going with you," he said.

"Me too!" Jane insisted."

"You have to stay with Rosswick. Join us later if you can," I said as I slid the door closed. Zane and I watched as the van pulled away.

21

SAVING THE MAGES

We watched as the van drove away until it was out of sight.

"He'll be ok," Dalia said as she turned back to her father.

"I hope so," I muttered, following behind her.

Tolsric looked around. "We must go now. Stay close and stay quiet."

I turned towards Zane. "Stay next to me," I said as we watched Tolsric wield his staff. He threw some black powder into the air, and it showered down like ash. Tolsric touched it with his staff as it floated down. It was like watching time freeze—the powder froze mid-flow and formed into a door. We watched as Tolsric opened it, allowing Dalia to enter first, then Zane and I, before he entered and shut the door behind him.

"Where are the others going?" Zane asked Tolsric.

"I have my own way into my realm," he said. "The others must head to the main gateway in order to enter or use their own secret entrances."

"Why couldn't you have just opened that from inside Hardgate?" I asked abruptly.

"These portals we create to get in and out of our realms are only accessible from the real world. Realm keepers prevent access to all realms using portals unless you're in the real world so criminals can't hop from realm to realm," Tolsric explained.

This one was a different type of portal, one that led to different areas in the realm of Valdekka. It brought us to a stone tunnel lit with torches as far as we could see. It was a tight squeeze, and we had to walk one by one as we followed Dalia. I stayed close to Zane, and Tolsric remained behind me. I started to get that eerie feeling in the pit of my stomach. There was a glow coming from the night sky, and the wind began blowing at us. We were reaching the end of the tunnel. Tolsric stopped us before reaching it.

"Wait!" he whispered aggressively. "We must wait here for the signal. The others have entered through different gateways all around Valdekka." Zane skimmed passed Dalia, hugging the wall to look out of the tunnel. He quickly slid back, making a shush motion.

"There are armored demons everywhere," he said.

"Wait for the signal," Tolsric said again, with anger this time. I pulled out my katana as we waited for a sign. An hour seemed to pass before we heard the loud siren of a bull horn echoing throughout the valley. We could see the soldiers as they loudly stomped and clanked past the narrow hall to organize their troops. They all appeared very tall, dressed in gold and silver armor.

"Wait, we mustn't be seen," Tolsric said as we were about to exit the tunnel. "We need to sneak into the fortress to kill Jarbin." We all nodded and silently squeezed out from the passage. Tolsric led us through the fortress corridors as we continued to hide from Jarbin's soldiers.

We seemed to be in a tower with lots of stairs that we followed up and around. Once we reached the top, Dalia said there was a bridge ahead that led to the castle where Jarbin should be. As we turned the corner, we were surprised by three soldiers standing guard. As they began to charge us, Dalia ran back to hide behind us. I swung my katana, slicing open the first soldier's abdomen below his armor chest plate. Zane swung his sword as well and began to fight with the second soldier. I watched the one I slaughtered drop to his knees and fall over. The third one jumped over Zane as he fought and ran straight towards me. Before I could raise my weapon, Tolsric held up his staff, and a beam shot from the tip. He struck the third soldier, blasting him back into a stone wall. Zane managed to take out the second demon soldier during the blast. We looked around to make sure the coast was clear. Dalia came out from behind a massive statue she had hidden behind and ran to her father.

"Let's go, quickly," I said, looking at Tolsric.

We ran across the bridge and into the main part of the castle. We could hear the screams from the battle outside as we crept through the halls. It was dark and dim inside. We were losing light, or what was left of it in the grey sky.

Tolsric led us through an empty banquet hall, stopping in front of the throne room and looking at us. "This is my battle," he said. "Go and free the slaves." Dalia looked at her father in distress before insisting that I go with him. He hugged her.

"This is my fight," he said. "Not hers. I must do this alone." He went in the throne room, shutting the door behind him. She began to cry as Zane and I pulled her away.

"Dalia, you have to show us where the slaves are kept," I said.

Dalia wiped the tears from her face. "Keep up," she said.

We followed her down a corridor. She kept taking us through large rooms that seemed to lead to others. Eventually, we were in another long hall that we rushed to get to the end of. She had us stop once we reached the end of it and pointed down to the back side of the castle. The end of the hall led to a large, rounded room with stairs on both sides, one set going up and one going down. The room had six rectangular windows that were taller than me. As I neared, I could see fields of prisoners locked inside a stone wall, chained to one another. I leaned through one of the broken panes, taking it all in. A tear fell down my cheek as I was overwhelmed with emotions, thinking only about my parents being somewhere out there amongst all of these people.

"Be careful," Zane said as I stood over the broken glass peering out.

"This is where the prisoners are kept in this realm," Dalia explained. "The walls around them are protected so they can't use their magic inside. They're chained together so no one can escape."

Zane peered down at the prisoners. "My god," he whispered before looking at me in fear. "How do you plan on getting them out, Anya? Seriously, do you even have a plan?" I stuttered, not knowing what to do or say.

"We're going to get killed here," he whispered aggressively. "We're surrounded by demons. This isn't going to end well for us."

"We're not here to get you killed. We're helping one another," Dalia said, trying to diffuse his anger. I walked over to Zane and reached up, grabbing his face with both hands, pulling him down towards me.

"We're here to free these people and find my parents, not abandon them in fear," I shouted angrily. I kissed his cold lips as he pulled away from me. "If you want to leave like a coward, then go! I will free these people and find my parents without you."

Zane stood there, confused, with blushing cheeks. "Well then, let's finish this," he said.

We snuck to the lower level through a stairway before the prison block. Dalia said there were black crystals called obsidian that kept mages from being able to use their powers inside the walls. We checked out the area and could see where we needed to knock the crystals down from the wall. Zane and Dalia were going to get two of the crystals from the east side of the wall, and I was to get the one from the west side.

We waited a bit till the coast cleared. When Jarbin's soldiers left the area, we snuck out from our hiding places. Dalia got the first one knocked down and Zane worked on his. I could see the one I needed to get, but it was up higher than I thought. I looked around for something to reach it with and noticed the window from the second level was close enough to jump from. I ran back to the stairwell and stopped to yell at Dalia to help Zane before running up.

Once I made it to the second level, there were two guards standing there. When they saw me, I turned and ran towards the window. They chased after me until I dove out the window. I caught myself on the brick ledge and managed to pull myself up. I could see the guards yelling and running to get down the stairwell. I scooted along the wall until I reached the crystal. I could see Zane had just knocked the second crystal from the wall as I kicked off the third. The prisoners were watching excitedly in anticipation. As the crystal fell, I could feel an overwhelming restraint lifted from me. I didn't notice how powerful the obsidian shield was until it was destroyed. The mages felt it too as they used their powers to free themselves from their shackles.

I looked back towards Zane and saw one of the guards had Dalia in his arms. He held a blade to her throat and was yelling something at Zane. Zane held his hands up and hesitantly got down on his knees as the other guard shoved him all the way to the ground. I jumped from the wall and ran in their direction. Before I could reach them, Tolsric and his army charged out and slaughtered the two guards.

"The reign of Jarbin is over!" Tolsric yelled, holding his staff up high.

I ran to Zane and helped him up, as Dalia ran to her father, hugging him and crying. We walked with Tolsric and a few of his people to the gate that was holding the prisoners.

"Some of you are meant to be in there, but a lot of you aren't," Tolsric said. "The reign of Jarbin is over, and you will all be pardoned." He pulled the gate open and freed the people.

I combed through the crowds of people, trying to find my parents. "Amoura, Asa! Amoura, Asa! Has anyone seen them?" I shouted.

Some men came and pulled Tolsric away as Zane and I continued to search. After several minutes, Dalia ran over to me, pulling at my arm. I leaned over to hear her because everyone was shouting and screaming as they fled.

"My father needs you," she shouted. "Come on." I grabbed Zane to get his attention, and he followed. Dalia led us up the stairs to the second level overlooking the prisoners, where her father and some men waited.

I approached cautiously as Tolsric looked at me with sadness.

"What do you need?" I asked.

"Your parents are no longer here, Anya," he said.

"What do you mean they're no longer here?" I asked, fearing the worst.

"We have been informed of a large move," Tolsric said. "Jarbin was running out of room here and needed to transfer many of the prisoners. Your parents were on the roster for Burning Hallows." He explained that it was a work camp for slaves in caves surrounded by magma that was nearly impenetrable.

"Take me there!" I pleaded with him.

"I must organize my people and restore order before I can leave again," he said.

"Please, you have to take me there," I begged. "It was our deal. You promised to free my parents."

"I will," he assured me. "If you just give me a day or two, I will show you how to get there and allow you access to the slave realm."

I looked at Zane, trying to hold back my tears when he came up and wrapped his arms around me.

"We were so close," I cried.

"Let's go home. We'll come back with the others when he's ready," Zane said." Tolsric handed Zane a map so that we could return to Valdekka.

Dalia said she would lead us back to the gateway we entered through. We watched the chaotic land of Valdekka restore power to its rightful leader. People were helping the injured and moving the deceased. It made me happy to see some of the people smiling and hugging loved ones once again. Some of these demons had been separated for months and could finally return home to their loved ones.

We reached the narrow passageway that led to the door.

"I'm sorry we couldn't find and free your parents yet," Dalia said, hugging me.

"I'll see you soon," I told her as she smiled and waved goodbye. Zane went in first, and I followed behind him until we reached the door at the end. Zane opened it and led us back to where we entered near the roadway. Once I closed the door, it slowly faded away.

"Guess we're not going back through there?" I asked. He looked at the map in his hand.

"Hopefully we can enter closer to home," he said. He grabbed my hand, and we began to walk in the direction of home.

22

FINDING HOME

We had been walking for hours. My feet hurt and body ached.

"It's getting dark," Zane said, looking at me. "We may need to find a place to camp for the night." I stared at him.

"How far before the next town?" I asked, hoping to sleep in a real bed.

He laughed at me. "Too far to walk tonight."

I groaned in frustration as Zane walked away from the road and towards the woods. I followed him through the tall grass till we reached the woods' edge, roughly a hundred yards from the street. There was barely enough light left in the day to see by when Zane began to make a small lean-to. I helped him drag over long skinny trees that he chopped down quickly with his hatchet. We laid them against a forked tree and bound them horizontally with vines I found nearby. We shoved some palm fronds between the vines to keep the wind off us. It wasn't perfect, but it protected our backs from the wind. Zane pulled out some matches that he had in his pocket, and I gathered some dry moss for kindling. He started the fire while I looked for some wood that was close to camp. Then he dragged a log over for us to sit on near the fire. It was a relief to have no fear of monsters hunting us here in the real world.

Sitting by the fire with Zane made me so relaxed. He made me feel better about finding my parents. We laughed about the funny things that happened to us and discussed the sad ones. We hoped Rosswick was doing better and couldn't wait to get back to see him and everyone else. It was getting cold, and I began to shiver, sliding closer to the fire. Zane moved over to me on the log and wrapped one arm over my shoulder to keep me warm. The temperature was dropping quickly; it felt like it was close to freezing already. He kept stoking the fire and adding more wood as time went by.

We eventually laid down near the fire, and Zane lay close enough to spoon me so we could stay warm. After about an hour of laying on the cold dirt tossing and turning I realized I couldn't sleep. Zane stroked my hair and rubbed my side, trying to comfort me back to sleep. Little did he know all I could think about was how he made me feel. I had to tell him. This was my chance while we were alone. Minutes had gone by before I felt brave enough to tell him how I felt.

"I need to tell you something I've been too afraid to say till now," I said quietly.

He pulled his head up. "You can tell me anything," he said, still holding me close.

I paused for a moment looking at the fire. "I really like you. Like really, really like you. I have ever since the first time I saw you when you returned from your last mission and walked in with the others." I turned my head back to look at him.

"I feel the same way about you, but I didn't want to say anything either," he said. "I figured you felt the same way when you kissed me in Valdekka."

I rolled over facing him, and we began to kiss. We began to roll over, entangling our bodies together. I pulled off his shirt. I had never felt this way before. I wanted him now more than ever.

He stopped me. "We can't do this."

"What's wrong?" I asked. He stood up and put his shirt back on.

"Back at the house, I'm your trainer. They won't understand, and Seth doesn't like us dating each other while we live at the house. He says it makes things complicated."

"Well then, we won't tell anyone," I said, walking to him.

"Then we need to take it slow," he said, hugging me.

"Ok, whatever you want," I said, smiling at him. We saw the sun beginning to rise and went to sit back near the fire. Zane sat on the log, and I sat on the other side. A few awkward minutes passed as I warmed my hands with the fire. Zane looked at me.

"Come here," he said with a grin on his face. I got up and went over, standing in front of him as we began to kiss again. I sat across his lap, and we watched the sunrise. It was magical. I had butterflies in my stomach all night but was relieved to finally tell him how he made me feel.

Once the sun was up, we coated the fire in sand and stomped out the ash before heading back to the main road. We held hands till we reached the road's edge and let go when we heard a car coming. Zane flagged them down and, to our surprise, it was our driver again. Seth had sent him back to wait for us. He unlocked the doors, and we began to get in.

"Glad I didn't have to wait as long for you guys this time," he said. We laughed and closed the door.

"How's Rosswick?" Zane asked. The driver wasn't sure; however, he did rush us home so we could find out. The drive felt much shorter on the way back, and things began to look more familiar. I had never felt so relieved to see the mansion peeking through the trees when we made the turn down the long drive. As we drove around the fountain, I was already opening my door and stepping out before he stopped.

I ran to the door, with Zane right behind me, rushed in, and shouted for Jane and Eddy as we ran through the house. I continued to shout out for anyone who was home. Passing the kitchen, I slid to a stop when I saw Eddy sitting at the breakfast bar. Zane rushed to him, asking how Rosswick was. Startled, Eddy nearly spit his cereal out.

"He's fine," Eddy said. "Seth got a few bullet fragments out and stopped the bleeding. He had surgery last night and is sleeping in the west wing." We both sighed in relief as Jane came around the corner. She leaned against the wall.

"Guess you didn't need our help?" she asked.

"Yes, we do," I quickly said. "My parents were moved to another place called Burning Hallows." She looked at me, stunned.

"Are you sure they're there. This isn't a trick?" she asked. "No one who goes to Burning Hallows leaves of their own free will."

"Dalia and Tolsric would never go back on their word," I told her, confused.

"We're here for you," Eddy interrupted. "Anything you need, we're in."

"Thanks, Eddy," I said. "Jane? Will you come and help us too?"

"We'll need to talk to Seth before making any hasty decisions," she said.

"Where is he?" I asked.

"He left last night after Rosswick's surgery. Hasn't been back since."

Zane left to check on Rosswick, and I waited with Eddy. After several minutes, I couldn't wait anymore. I needed to get my mind off everything.

I got up and said I needed a shower.

"Yes, you do," Jane said quickly, making a joke. "You look and smell like you've been living with Bigfoot."

I was so tired, I just walked to my room, wondering where Seth had gone. Once in my room, it almost felt like I was back home. It was nice to see something familiar again. There were so many times I felt like we weren't going to make it home. I wondered how my mom was and if she was doing any better than myself. The thoughts of the torture my biological parents were going through haunted me deeply. Knowing I had to wait a day or more before being able to rescue them sickened me.

I glanced around the room before gathering some clothes out of the drawer and dragging my tired self to the shower. I set my clothes on the shelf near the shower and turned on the water. Feeling the water to make sure it was warm, I climbed in. It felt so good to wash off the grime of the past few days. I dried off and got dressed before looking for the others again.

I walked around to find Jane as I dried my hair. I made it to the living room where I was surprised by Seth sitting on the couch. I rushed over to him to tell him everything that happened, but he stopped me to tell me that Jane had already told him.

"Will you come with us to Burning Hallows?" I asked.

"I will not be going with you. Jane, Eddy, and Zane may go if they wish," he said looking at me with a serious stare. "But Rosswick will not be well enough to go."

I thanked him for everything and took the towel off my head. "My parents will be so thankful."

"I like what you've done with your hair," he said, smiling.

"It wasn't a choice," I explained.

"An archmage is a true gift of power and leadership. Use it well as you lead people in life."

"Lead people where?" I asked.

"One day you will be like your parents and lead other mages into the future," he said, chuckling. I thanked him again and went to go look for Zane.

Jane rushed down the hall. "When are we going to be leaving?" she asked.

"We need to find Zane. He knows where we're going since he has the map," I said.

Eddy came from around the corner eating something else. "He's checking on Rosswick," he said around the food in his mouth. We went to the west wing to find him. As we neared the room, we could see Zane at Rosswick's bedside. It was hard to see Rosswick laying there with all the tubes coming out of him.

"Is Rosswick awake?" I asked Zane.

"Not yet," Zane said, not looking away from Rosswick. He sounded so sad. I was about to say something when he continued. "We are like brothers. I've known him since I was ten. His family took me in when no one else would." I walked over and put my hand on his shoulder.

"He's going to be ok," I said. I told him we needed to get ready to go, and that Seth would keep a close eye on Rosswick. Zane still had not taken his eyes away from him.

"I know, I'm coming," he mumbled. I walked away, leaving him with Rosswick a little longer. Walking away, I saw Jane still standing nearby.

"Come on, Jane," I said.

Jane and I walked back to the kitchen to tell Eddy to get ready.

"I need to do a couple things," Jane said. "I'll be right back."

Eddy looked at me as Jane walked away. "Well, that was odd," he said.

I laughed. "Everything Jane does is odd." We laughed about it, and I told him to go get ready as I went to my room to get my bag packed.

As I walked in my room, I let out a large sigh of nervousness. I had never felt so ready for a battle yet so scared to save and meet my parents. I grabbed some clothes and stuffed them in my bag. Looking at the mirror above my dresser I hardly recognized myself. So much had changed and I feared what Mom would say when I could finally see her again.

I sat on my bed and just stared at the picture on the wall. It was a large owl looking back at me. Lost in my thoughts, I noticed it was getting late in the day. Suddenly, Zane popped in.

"You ready?" he shouted eagerly.

I hopped up and snatched my bag from my bed. "Let's go."

ABOUT THE AUTHOR

Mercedes Hubert has been married to her loving and supportive husband since 2018. She has a Bachelor of Science degree in Criminal Justice. Graduating *magna cum laude* in 2020. She doesn't have any kids of her own but has two wonderful step kids that test her patience. She also has the love of her senior Chihuahua Rex, and her new Bengal kitty Luna "the lunatic" to motivate her each day. She enjoys going to the zoo or getting away to game/anime conventions when she has free time.